PRAISE FOR STEVEN-ELLIOT ALTMAN

An erotic and lyrical fantasy thriller, aptly set in the city of lost angels.

— POPPY Z. BRITE, AUTHOR OF *LOST SOULS*
AND *EXQUISITE CORPSE*

In *Severed Wings*, Altman delivers a thrilling roller coaster ride, plunging us headlong into dark territories fraught with unexpected pivots and twists.

— STEPHEN SUSCO, SCREENWRITER OF *THE
GRUDGE*

Steve Altman's *Severed Wings* is a tour de force of the Weird. Eat of the fruit and take a truly mesmerizing trip through a glass darkly. I did, and I can't wait to do it again.

— NANCY HOLDER, *NEW YORK TIMES*
BESTSELLING AUTHOR OF THE WICKED
SERIES, WRITTEN WITH DEBBIE VIGUIE

SEVERED WINGS

SEVERED WINGS

STEVEN-ELLIOT ALTMAN

WFP
WORDFIRE PRESS

EBook ISBN: 978-1-68057-035-9
Trade Paperback ISBN: 978-1-68057-034-2
Hardcover ISBN: 978-1-68057-036-6

Cover design by Janet McDonald
Cover artwork images by John Jude Palencar
Kevin J. Anderson, Art Director
Published by
WordFire Press, LLC
PO Box 1840
Monument CO 80132
Kevin J. Anderson & Rebecca Moesta, Publishers
WordFire Press eBook Edition 2020
WordFire Press Trade Paperback Edition 2020
WordFire Press Hardcover Edition 2020
Printed in the USA
Join our WordFire Press Readers Group for
sneak previews, updates, new projects, and giveaways.
Sign up at wordfirepress.com

❀ Created with Vellum

This book is dedicated to some soul who inspired it, who shall not be named, and may understand why. Don't worry, it's not you.

Special thanks to my brilliant editor, Patrick Merla, as well as my chief sounding boards Michael K. Thomas and Cathy Thomas, my tenacious agent, Tim Travaglini, and ingenious manager, Grace Ledding; my faithful translator, Nathalie Japsar; my precious first readers, Dawn Emery Thorne, Benjamin Davis, Rachel Bieber, Jessica Sattelberger, Shannon Motherway, Julie Marsh, Lourdes Navarro, and Mindy Yale for your insightful notes; Brianna Winner, Christopher Paolini, Dorian Hannaway, Diane DeKelb-Rittenhouse, and especially Nicole Powers for your priceless, compassionate input; Gordon Watson, for helping me get the police matters right; Lori Collins, for helping me get the mountain-climbing matters right; John Jude Palencar, for the breathtaking cover art; Kevin Anderson and Rebecca Moesta, for years of friendship, encouragement, and for taking a chance on this strange little book; and to Nancy Holder, Stephen Susco, and Poppy Z. Brite, for providing thoughtful feedback and inspiring jacket quotes. Did I miss anyone? Hope not.

PROLOGUE

y agent promised it was going to be the party to end all parties. It may be the only promise he made me that came true.

Felicia and I got lost on our way before doubling back along the steep, winding road threading the Hollywood Hills. Eventually, we found the place. The party was black tie, and I was wearing a John Varvatos suit I'd borrowed from my best friend, Marty. Felicia was poured into the gorgeous Vera Wang dress I'd given her on Valentine's Day, which she'd been saving for a special occasion.

I was twenty-six years old, in the best mental and physical shape of my life, with a great apartment, great friends, and madly in love with the best girl ever. Two days ago, I'd been deemed a "handsome, talented, young up-and-comer" by *Variety*, in a column about the network series in which I'd landed a starring role. A mention like that brings you heat in this town, and a ticking clock marking the time you have to sell your sizzle and attach yourself to bigger and better film and TV projects before the heat moves on to someone else. It was prime time to make bank on me, and my agent wanted me seen. He'd grudgingly agreed to let my girlfriend come along because Felicia and I had made a pact to achieve success together—although that's not what I'd told him when I insisted on bringing her.

Felicia was a beautiful girl with a big heart, dimples that wouldn't quit, and huge prospects. Slender to the degree that Hollywood had decreed fashionable for the day, but with enough curves to get her into the right places, a girl-next-door innocence, and a high-powered manager who kept producers from making the wrong moves with her. Twenty-four years old, she'd already been signed by a premier modeling agency and done several national commercials that brought in solid residuals. She'd come to Los Angeles from Minnesota three years ago, on her birthday. Shortly thereafter, we were cast in the same play. We'd been inseparable ever since.

We sat in the car at the foot of a hidden driveway, behind a long line of Mercedes and BMWs waiting for a valet. I lifted Felicia's hand and brushed a kiss across her fingers, slipping my free hand beneath the thigh-high slit of her gown. She protested briefly before her laugh became a moan, and quickly had my zipper down and the length of me urgent against her own hand. A gasp of pleasure, after which she lay back against the car seat, cheeks flushed, breathing erratic, trembling as I spoke low in her ear, telling her how beautiful she was, how precious to me, coaxing her toward a blistering peak, holding her as her body shuddered into climax, soothing her as the storm passed and calm returned. She still held me in her grasp, clever fingers, teasing nails, delicious pressure. I was about tell her to reach for a tissue from the glove compartment when I saw the valet coming toward us. I groaned and told her to stop.

More laughter as I straightened my clothes and assured Felicia her makeup remained flawless as she adjusted her panties and rearranged her skirt, her eyes flashing promises for later. I licked each of my fingers in response. She handed me the sanitizer just in time—the valet was almost at our door.

Felicia clutched my hand, radiating pleasure (and not only from the last few moments) as I helped her from the car. A few A-list celebrities joined us as we stood before a pretty hostess flanked by two burly security guards. She inspected our IDs, checked our names off the list on her clipboard, and directed us all to go up the hill and follow the path through the wooded area. The path was lined with candles, their glow hardly evident yet due to the spectacular sunset through the trees illuminating the glass walls of a modern, multimillion-dollar home landscaped into the hillside.

Party sounds beckoned us through the open doors into a palatial foyer with marble floors. We strode past walls lined with floor-to-ceiling film posters from silent films and a room where a group of well-dressed kids snorted coke off a grand piano, to the rear of the house (also walled in glass), and outside to the main event—a vast patio complete with a cliffside reflecting pool and a breathtaking bird's-eye view of Los Angeles.

We made our way through the bustling crowd seeded with Hollywood climbers to the bar on the opposite side of the pool.

"Brandon, there you are!"

My agent materialized out of a group of elegantly dressed people I didn't know.

"So glad you could make it, Felicia," he lied.

"Good to see you, too," she lied back, then went off to work the party on her own as previously agreed (we often doubled our coverage that way at social events).

"There's a ton of people here you need to meet," my agent said as if nothing had happened. "Including that hot shit writer-director I told you about who just got his feature green-lit at Paramount. Put you up for it this morning, but didn't wanna get your hopes up. Six figures. Shoots in Morocco. Do us both a favor and don't fuck up."

Cocktails in hand, we made the rounds. I was doing my best to impress everyone while my agent lauded my series as must-see

TV. The flow of alcohol was constant, lubricating the deals being brokered all around us. That didn't faze me. In this town, holding your liquor well is as important a skill as any acquired in acting class. My agent seemed pleased with my performance; by midnight he'd left me on my own with a warning not to stay too late or—Heaven forbid—say or do anything stupid. By then I was ready to call it a night myself.

I downed my last drink and searched for Felicia, dimly recollecting her whispering in my ear at some point she'd decided to head out early, called a taxi, and would see me later—urging me to go do my thing, stay as long as I wanted—but I was fuzzy on that, and if it had happened then it couldn't have been more than a few moments earlier.

I stood at the edge of the reflecting pool, scanning for her among the thinning crowd lingering by the heat lamps, smoking various substances. I peered at the house with a growing sense of apprehension.

That's when I felt a tug at my pant leg.

I looked down to discover a cute little curly-haired girl of perhaps six or seven staring up at me. She was wearing some kind of shimmery costume which included a pair of gracefully curved wings. They were made of large, soft feathers that gave them a puffy look, and they shimmered as much as the cloth of her robe.

"Hello," I said. "Do you live here?"

No, she shook her head.

"Are you a bird?" I teased.

"Not a bird ..." she replied, curtly, clearly displeased. Her voice had a warbled, distorted echo to it that alarmed me, and she glared at me with a penetrating stare so uncannily mature and knowing that it made my blood run cold. "An angel!"

Suddenly, my vision swam, and everything around me began to move in slow motion. I felt a sense of inertia, like the ground was moving beneath me, slipping out from under me, and fought to keep my balance.

The last thing I remember is a pair of blinding twin spot-lights beaming out at me from inside the house, a screeching sound like tires skidding, and a car smashing through the glass wall straight at me.

CHAPTER 1

I woke up to the harsh light of a hospital room and the sound of crying. My mother sat hunched over beside my bed clutching rosary beads. She looked haggard, her clothes unpressed as if she'd slept in them.

"Mom ..." My voice cracked. I could barely form the sound.

She gasped and leapt up, reaching for me, but there was nowhere to put her hands. My arms and legs were held aloft by a three-dimensional maze of wires, tubes, and hangers.

"You've been in a very bad car accident," she whispered. "God saved you. Father Tom has been in to see you and says it's a miracle you survived."

She probably would have gone on in that vein if the doctors hadn't come in. They told me I'd suffered acute fractures to the lower thoracic and upper lumbar regions of my spinal cord. Neural trauma. I couldn't quite follow it all through the haze of morphine—a grogginess that made me feel detached from reality, from the room, from the tubes and wires and beeping monitors, from whatever it was they were trying to explain to me.

Slowly, I came to understand—seeing their faces, letting their words sink in—the full impact of what they were telling me.

They had to tell me several times, and even demonstrate, before I understood completely that I could not feel or move my legs.

I'd been in a head-on collision on the 405 freeway that had severed my spine in one horrific crush of glass and steel, leaving me paralyzed from the waist down. My only consolation was that the drunken frat boy who'd crashed into me was no longer with us.

Felicia camped out by my bedside throughout my hospital stay, tolerating my misplaced rage as day after day, somber specialists came back with the same bleak prognosis. "Medical science keeps advancing. There is a chance you will walk again someday, son. Hang in there, Brandon."

Six months later my condition had not improved, despite endless hours of physical therapy and my mother's unceasing prayers. I was living with my parents again; a helpless cripple dependent on their charity, convinced that my whole life lay behind me, wishing I were dead.

I'd sit in my wheelchair, which I'd christened the "cripple wagon," and stare in the full-length mirror on the back of my bedroom door—the only mirror in the house low enough for me to see myself. My useless legs remained senseless against the steel leg supports, my feet dead weights on the footrests. My hands, half covered by leather gloves that left my fingers bare, clutched the metal rims of the rubber wheels. My arms by now had grown twice as muscular as they'd been before the accident. The result of all the physical therapy, and my refusal to let anyone help me with the chair.

Ironically, after all I'd been through my face still matched my headshots. My agent sent me out on two auditions. Although the studios are legally supposed to be blind to handicaps, it was clear to me that both casting directors took one look at my wheelchair and decided that I "wasn't right" for the parts before I even read my lines.

I was so upset after the second failure that I called the Screen Actors Guild to report discrimination. The woman I spoke to told me I could file a complaint, and if I proved it the casting people would be fined. Then she explained what would probably happen. I might be offered a single episode walk-on part—no pun intended—to shut me up. More likely, I'd be quietly blacklisted, allowed to audition but never hired. Seeing my true calling slipping beyond my grasp forever somehow felt worse than being sentenced to life in a wheelchair. Faced with the harsh reality of my situation, I told her to forget it.

As I was about to hang up, she asked, "But you are taking advantage of your disability benefits, right?" She told me she knew of a reasonably priced apartment in West Hollywood for which I qualified.

That was the day I decided I'd had enough humiliation. It was time to make some changes.

The Villa Rosa is a four-story white stone apartment building between Fairfax and Orange Grove Avenue on Sunset Boulevard. With its prominent black fire escapes, it looks like it belongs on some side street in Brooklyn rather than on the main drag in Los Angeles. Hearing that I was an actor, the pudgy, sweat-stained rental agent who showed me the place enthused that it had housed a lot of aspiring talents who went on to have highly successful, often tragic careers, chief among them James Dean.

I belong here, I thought.

She fumbled out two sets of keys from her purse at the arched black iron security gate.

"The buzzer links to your phone," she said, indicating the tenant directory as she wiped sweat off her forehead. This was common now for LA apartment buildings, replacing the old intercom system; you'd answer your phone instead, then press 9 to buzz someone in. "Otherwise, it's remained pretty much the same as when it was built as a hotel back in 1928," she added. "It's sort of like going back in time."

She held open the gate, and I wheeled my cripple wagon past her into a sunny courtyard on either side of which rose the two wings of the U-shaped building. Like an eager tour guide, she proceeded to describe in detail what made the Villa Rosa "special" while we moved along a path of paving stones bordered by palm trees stretching all the way up the sides of the building and crowning the rooftops with their luxuriant fronds.

"Those trees were planted by one of the tenants a long time ago," the agent said. "Can you believe it?"

The path widened at the end around a sculpted bronze fountain centered within an octagonal pool faced with Spanish tiles. Koi swam in the water. A few feet beyond the fountain was the entrance to the lobby, whose antique wood doors, the agent told me, were always left open.

The lobby had a row of metal mailboxes on our right and a long, rudimentary wood bench on the left, low against the wall. The floor was terra-cotta tiling. Dominating the lobby was a colorful floor-to-ceiling stained-glass window facing outward to the courtyard. It depicted a wooden ship with full-blown, broad-striped sails at sea with the words *Villa Rosa* in red block letters emblazoned beneath it. A circular wrought iron chandelier with eleven miniature shades hung from the ceiling.

Off the lobby was the ancient wood-paneled elevator, which fortunately accommodated my wide wheels. The agent mentioned that there was a laundry room in the basement. We ascended to the fourth floor.

"There are actually two apartments vacant on this floor," she said as we turned a corner to our right after exiting the elevator. "But only one of them is designated ... handicap accessible."

I followed her along a dimly lit hallway at the far end of which French doors had been left open, revealing the black metal fire escape. Shafts of sun, like light at the end of a tunnel, reflected softly on the rustic plaster walls. Exposed black iron piping spanned the ceiling from one end to the other. A well-worn carpet runner with a leaf-and-flower pattern stretched the length of hallway, with heavily varnished plank hardwood flooring exposed along the edges. The agent pointed out the narrow black metal plates bolted to the floor at irregular intervals, explaining that they were earthquake support braces, installed just after the 1994 Northridge quake.

The apartment was a large studio with exposed brick walls and, once again, plank hardwood floors with seemingly haphazardly placed earthquake braces. The small caster wheels of my cripple wagon bumped as I rolled over them.

"Check out the view," the agent suggested.

Through three tall windows facing Sunset Boulevard, I could see the Hollywood Hills to the northeast, with Griffith Observatory in the distance looking like a small Parthenon atop Mt. Olympus. A corner window overlooked Orange Grove Avenue, with downtown Los Angeles sprawling to the southeast. All of the windows had wrought iron security grilles with heart-shaped motifs.

The agent directed my attention back to the apartment's interior. "You're gonna love this," she promised. She led me across the living room to what appeared to be a polished wooden armoire, recessed into the wall—then reached to unlatch it—and demonstrated that is was in fact a hidden, queen-size Murphy bed, which lowered effortlessly into place.

"Fun, right? Most of the studios have them," she said. "Murphy beds were commonplace back in the day. They allow for more functional living space."

A kitchen area was separated somewhat from the main room by a counter, with cabinets and refrigerator shelves all low enough for me to reach from my wheelchair. The shower and toilet in the bathroom, down a short hallway, were also cripple friendly. The place came furnished. All the furniture was custom-made, left behind by the previous tenant, who had also been wheelchair bound, and had died there.

I knew this because I discovered an embossed prayer card from his memorial service peeking out from beneath some dusty papers which had been left sitting atop the overfilled trash bin.

Died peacefully in his sleep at his apartment on ...

My breath caught as I read the date of death.

I had to read it again to make sure my mind wasn't playing tricks on me. I was aware that the agent continued to speak, but her voice grew suddenly distant and unintelligible as my realization solidified.

He'd died on the night of my accident.

Chills ran through me and left tingling gooseflesh up and down my arms. What were the chances of that?

I turned the card over to reveal a familiar painting of a haloed angel, head bowed, wings extended, hands steepled in prayer.

This must be where I'm supposed to die, too, I thought. *A fitting tomb for a willing occupant.*

I realized the agent was hovering over me, her face a mask of concern. "Forgive me, did I forget to mention the last tenant passed away here? To be honest, he wasn't the first. John Drew Barrymore passed on here as well. He was an actor turned acting coach who operated out of the building. Coached James Dean and Steve McQueen right here in the apartment. Word has it he struggled with drugs and alcohol his entire career."

Now, my relationship with God had grown complicated since the accident, to say the least. But these were signs that were impossible for me to ignore.

"I'll take it," I told her.

About a week later, the strategic withdrawal from my prior life was nearly complete. My parents hired movers to transport my belongings and stocked the fridge. I had cable, Internet, Netflix, and menus from every eatery that delivered food to the area. A maid was scheduled to arrive once per week. Through the pity of several government agencies and my labor union, just enough money filled my bank account each month to cover my few expenses. The next order of business, before I could get down to proper grieving for my shattered existence, was breaking up with Felicia.

Before the accident, we'd planned to move in together, get married, and eventually have kids, meanwhile reaching the height of our careers and stowing away tons of cash. None of that was going to happen now, at least not in my case, yet still Felicia stuck by me.

After the hospital, she'd spent every other night with me at my parents' house. She had a life of her own of course—friends to visit, a dog to walk, auditions to attend. I understood. At first we kept up hope that the doctors were wrong, that my spinal injury would not permanently inhibit my ability to perform in bed. Lack of ability did not mean lack of desire. If anything, I was hungrier for her now than I had been before the accident. Like a phantom limb, my erection made itself known every time Felicia and I got close. But paralyzed from the waist down means exactly that. Despite my brain's insistence that I was ready to go, my body was not on the same page, or even in the same book.

The first time we made the attempt, we were naked together, kissing. I could *feel* myself hard and ready for her. For a few seconds, I exulted in the miracle I'd been given. I looked down at my flaccid, useless flesh. That may have been the most unbearable moment of my life.

After that, we'd tried everything from pornography to Viagra to a particularly mortifying attempt with a vacuum pump. Each failure introduced me to new depths of despair. But my fingers still worked, and so did my mouth; despite my poorly hidden frustration, I mastered both techniques to a degree I never would have otherwise. It worked for a time. Felicia's compassion and patience seemed endless. "I don't need all that other stuff," she said, and we both needed to believe it.

But soon after I'd moved into the Villa Rosa, I'd built up the courage to face the truth and cast off the emotional cushion she provided. My girlfriend had the yearnings of a fit young woman in her prime. I had those yearnings, too, and had been cursed with an injury that rendered my body unable to service either of our considerable drives any longer. We'd lie in bed, naked, engaging in the poor imitation of the love we'd once made so enthusiastically. I'd see the wanton look in her eyes I knew well, and I just couldn't take it.

And I'll admit I was guilty of checking her text messages and knew she was resisting the attentions of a guy she'd been partnered with for scene study in her acting class. I'd met him once or twice before the accident, and it made me jealous as hell for a while. Felicia was a good girl. I imagined her fending him off, out of pity and loyalty to me. "I'm not ready yet. It's too soon. He's crippled. Be patient, it's not like we're still having sex." That was no way for her to live.

So, as the last act of control I could muster over my past, I picked a fight and ended our relationship before her hormones inevitably did.

I accused her of sleeping with her manager. She vehemently denied it.

"If you're not sleeping with him, you'll be sleeping with someone else sooner or later," I countered. "I know what you like, Felicia. I can't provide it anymore, and what we are doing certainly doesn't satisfy me."

The fight escalated. Foul words were spoken and we both shed many tears. In the end, we assured each other we'd be friends again eventually, and Felicia gathered up the few belongings she kept at my apartment—a toothbrush, a hair dryer, a coat from the closet—and walked out the door without looking back. I wheeled myself to the fire escape to watch her get into her car and drive off for the last time, then rolled back into the apartment feeling empty, yet relieved.

I'd like to say the breakup was altruistic on my part, that I couldn't bear to keep denying my girlfriend a normal sex life.

The truth is, Felicia had become for me a mirror of what my life once had been. Staying with her was a constant, painful reminder of my emasculation. I couldn't handle it. And I couldn't stomach the thought of her being with anyone else. My vanity and ego wouldn't stand for it. I've admitted this to myself. In my defense, I told myself I didn't want my handicap to extend to her, that our relationship was destroyed by tragic circumstances and she was better off without me. I prayed she'd find someone who would treat her as she deserved.

Our two headshots had been mounted in frames on the living room wall. I left hers up for several days, then finally had to take it down because it was too painful to look at. Ironically, as I wriggled the nail out to remove her headshot, mine slipped off the wall and hit the floor, shattering the glass. I cleaned up the shards, trashed both pictures, spackled the nail holes, and refreshed the paint.

Next I went about exorcising friends from my life. For a few, it was as simple as not returning their calls or failing to answer emails. Others required blocking or deleting from Facebook. Losing the more persistent ones took work. Finally, I changed my cell phone number and deleted all my social media accounts. I assume word got around that I wanted to be left alone.

The last of them was Marty, my best friend since junior high school. He persuaded my folks to give him my address. (Who could blame them? I had not taken their calls in weeks.) I had no choice but to buzz him in when I answered my phone and discovered he was downstairs at the Villa Rosa gate. He was clearly surprised when I opened my apartment door.

"Jesus, when was the last time you shaved, Brandon?" he said. "You look like hell."

"It's good to see you, too," I lied.

I'd dimmed the lights in my studio while he was on his way up, and drawn all the curtains. Now I wheeled myself to the cabinet to get a pair of clean glasses, uncorked a bottle of wine for us to share, put on a CD of Tibetan monks chanting, and lit a candle for dramatic effect, setting the stage for the murder of our friendship.

"Who else knows you're here?" I began. "Please tell me you haven't given my address out to the old crew."

"Of course not," Marty said. "But people are worried about you. Including your folks."

"Why are they worried?" I asked, sipping my wine. "Do they think I can't take care of myself because I'm alone and crippled?"

I could tell Marty was nervous. The stem of his wineglass trembled in his hand; I noticed perspiration on his upper lip.

"No, no," he stammered. "People still love you, man. We can't understand why you don't want to see us."

I detested myself for what I was about to do as I called on my acting skills and allowed just a trace of disgust to appear on my face, careful not to let the demon out too fast. Poor Marty was merely an innocent audience member to my self-destruction.

"You don't understand," I echoed him savagely. "You can't fathom why I'd want to detach myself from everything that reminds me of who I used to be? I see you, and I remember running across the field during lacrosse practice. I see Sarah, and I remember rock climbing in Yosemite. I can't walk or run or climb or drive anymore. I can't act, or have a normal relationship. Forget about having children—*I can't screw!*" I was shouting now. "I'm done, Marty. And I don't need you coming here to remind me. So take your pity and fuck off!"

I was good—as good as if I'd rehearsed this unpleasant little scene.

"Brandon, I ..." He was unable to continue. Tears welled in his eyes. He took a few halfhearted sips of his wine. He stared at the floor.

We sat in silence for about a minute. Finally, he got up, his chair making an unnerving screech as he pushed it back, and showed himself out.

I locked the door behind him, wondering if I'd made a

mistake. Marty was my best friend. But it was better this way. My past was dead. From now on, there would be no more painful reminders of who I'd been or my promising future, no one to compare me to my former virile self. From now on, I would only let new people into my world, people who'd never known me as anything other than a cripple.

I finished the bottle of wine while I watched that old Stephen King movie where the guy's car is possessed by a demon.

CHAPTER 2

*A*fter that none of my old friends tried to contact me, which suited me fine. Eventually, even my parents stopped calling. The only interactions I had were casual pleasantries with delivery boys, the maid (who spoke no English), and my fellow inmates at the Villa Rosa, every one of them unwittingly cast as a walk-on character in my stewing melodrama.

. Due to proximity, I saw more of my neighbor in the apartment adjacent to mine than anyone else. Ray was tall, lanky, jovial, with thick lips, pitted skin, and a quick wit. He was also a transvestite, and was constantly changing wigs and shades of eye makeup to match his garish drag. Ray kept strange hours, stranger company, and typically was too drunk to carry on a conversation with me whenever we met for a moment in our hallway. "Hey there, Ironside," he'd say when he saw me roll by, then laugh to himself. I caught glimpses into his apartment, a sea of plush red fuzzy furniture and two ever-mewing Siamese cats whose names I never knew.

The night after Felicia left, I invited him to my place. We got stoned over a bottle of wine, which loosened both our tongues. Ray told me he'd heard muffled pieces of the fight, and asked me what had happened. I gave him all the grisly details of why I'd driven her away, including that I no longer had a functioning sex organ.

"I feel for you, baby," he responded. "I'm saving up to have mine removed. Caused me nothing but heartache."

I struck up an awkward platonic friendship with a girl I met in the laundry room on several occasions. Bethany lived below me. She let me use her fabric softener, even though I really didn't need it. She was moderately cute, but not the type I would have pursued back when I was still capable of closing the deal. Her nose was too thin and her hips too narrow, and I never had a thing for redheads. We'd established a bi-weekly ritual of ordering takeout from various restaurants and adjourning from the basement to her third-floor fire escape while our clothes were drying. Villa Rosa tenants referred to the fire escapes as balconies because that's how we used them. I'd sit in my wheel-chair in the open French doors while Bethany plopped herself onto the top step of the metal stairs leading down to the next story. She was really into the building's history and informed me the actress Shelley Winters lived here for a time and in her memoir detailed how she was having a tryst with Marlon Brando when her boyfriend showed up at the door—forcing Brando to climb out a window and down the rear fire escape! One time I asked her what she did for a living, and she told me without fuss that she worked as an escort. It was the simplest way to earn enough to pay her way through college. She didn't often tell people, she said, but she felt she could trust me; I don't know why. I figured it was a combination of the fact that I never hit on her, coupled with my presumed physical weakness from being in a wheelchair.

On the first floor lived an elderly woman named Gladys, who had taken it upon herself to tend the flowers in the courtyard, even though the building employed a gardener. Gladys always wore the same flowered bathrobe and slippers, her white hair more often than not done up in old-fashioned pink plastic curlers. Her eyes flittered back and forth uncontrollably whenever she spoke to me—or perhaps I should say *at* me—in a manner that left me unsure if she realized I was actually there. "I do hope you'll be feeling better soon," she commented at our first meeting, observing my wheelchair. I found this rather odd, considering she had no idea as to the extent of my injury. I was going to say so, but she'd already resumed her pruning and was no longer looking at me. I watched her thin fingers at work plucking away dead roses. Then she added, seemingly to herself, "Everyone who moves into the Villa Rosa comes in need of healing. Yes, they do."

Later, I asked Ray about her. He told me Gladys was once a very famous actress who'd starred in dozens of films, although offhand he couldn't recall a single title.

The rest of the tenants were middle-aged actors who didn't quite have "the look" or quite fit a "type," writers who hadn't yet found their own "voice," or musicians who would probably never earn anything from their own compositions but made just enough to live on by performing other people's music. It seemed each of them had come from somewhere in Middle America to seek fame and glory in Los Angeles and had found an affordable "rest stop" at the Villa Rosa on their way to Beverly Hills and their names in lights—or back home in disgrace, whichever came first. Like me, many of them were Section 8 tenants, our fixed rents subsidized by the city, the landlord having been mandated to provide apartments to persons designated as low income: senior citizens, people with disabilities, and my neighbors. We all considered ourselves lucky to be living there.

Ray, Bethany, and Gladys were pretty much the only souls I interacted with when I chose to interact with anyone, which was rare. My preferred activity was sleeping. I tried for at least sixteen hours per day, often using pills obligingly prescribed by my doctor. Since the accident, I had become somewhat adept at lucid dreaming. In sleep I had a life. I could walk, run, dance, and make love. I highly preferred this to my waking existence. And I took comfort in the knowledge that one day even that curse would end.

Three months after I moved into the Villa Rosa, I was rolling down the hall toward the elevator with my rent check to deposit it in the designated mailbox slot on the first floor. I noticed that the door to the apartment across the hall from me was ajar; inside, I could just make out several cardboard boxes. I presumed that there was finally a new occupant. But I did not see anyone.

When I returned to my apartment, I locked myself in, feeling unusually apprehensive. Having someone new across the hall was major casting over which I had no say. I prayed that whoever it was would be quiet and not have a dog. What if it was a Hollywood type, with noisy friends arriving at all hours? Or a musician who never stopped practicing? Or, worse yet, a drug dealer whose junkie clients would pound on my door by mistake?

It was days before I saw my new neighbor for the first time, at about 2:00 AM. Ray's television was on low next door. I heard something heavy drop in the hallway.

The one thing in my apartment that had not been modified to suit someone in a wheelchair was the peephole in the front door. This hadn't bothered me before, but now I felt a desperate need to see my new neighbor, and it wouldn't do for me to suddenly roll out my door at that early hour of the morning. Besides, I wasn't dressed. In my cripple wagon I was effectively four feet tall. How could I get myself up to the peephole?

Then I remembered the phone books in my closet. I'd dumped them there because they were too big and heavy to stuff in my garbage, then kept forgetting to have the maid discard them. After all this time, I finally had a use for them.

I wheeled myself to the closet to retrieve them, stacking the three phone books on my lap and rolling back to the door. Now came the tricky part. I put on my chair brakes and lowered the books, then myself, to the floor, then stacked the books on the seat of the chair. Next, I laboriously climbed on top, doing my best to keep the books from slipping out from under my rear end, and wedged myself in the chair against the door. It was frustrating—and rather infantilizing, considering the result—but I'd effectively turned my wheelchair into a high chair and raised myself to eye level with the peephole.

I peered out from my precarious perch—only to find that the hallway was empty, the door across the hall shut tight. My efforts had been wasted.

Then I noticed a crack of light at the bottom of my neighbor's door, and decided to wait to see if the door reopened, fancying myself a young Sherlock Holmes. There I perched, feeling foolish, yet unable to move away because it was simply too complicated. I lost track of time, and may have dozed off intermittently. Finally the door opened.

Out stepped a dark-haired, bearded young man I guessed to be close to my age, wearing dark jeans and a winter jacket with a fur-lined hood. Before the door closed again behind him, I glimpsed stacks of large cardboard moving boxes; there seemed to be more than I'd noticed earlier. He made his way toward the elevator. I decided to turn in, rather than continue perching there with the idiotic hope of finding out anything more right then.

I maneuvered the phone books out from under me, cursing the low hallway lighting for not allowing me to see him better. The best I could tell was that he appeared rugged and had broad shoulders and a sturdy physique. His coat struck me as odd. It looked far too warm for LA, especially at this time of year. Granted, it got cold here at night, but not cold enough to require fur. And how had he managed to move in all those cartons without my noticing?

The next day I put in a request with the building manager for a lower peephole and brighter hall lights, saying that the current batch didn't provide enough illumination for me to navigate the hall well at night. The maintenance man changed the lights that afternoon, and promised the peephole had been ordered and would be installed at my desired height as soon as it arrived; complaints from cripples tend to get handled quickly in this town.

A few days later, I ran into Bethany in the laundry room. Over coffee and sandwiches she picked up for us from Bristol Farms grocery next door, I asked if she'd seen my new neighbor yet.

"I met him a couple nights ago," she said, "when I got home from seeing a client. Doesn't talk much, but oh my God! I'd fuck him in a heartbeat."

"So you think he's good-looking?" I asked rhetorically.

"Obviously you haven't seen him," she retorted. "If you had, you wouldn't be kidding me like that."

I didn't respond.

"Not that I'd stand a chance in hell with him," she continued. "He's got a girlfriend."

"You met her, too?"

"Not exactly. She was sitting in his Jeep while he unloaded boxes at the curb. Must be a model or actress—she's drop-dead gorgeous. Has the biggest eyes I've ever seen. Stared me down like a hawk."

"Is she living with him?"

"You tell me. You live across the hall from him."

"I'll let you know, if and when I find out," I said, hoping I sounded indifferent to Bethany.

"You do that," she said with a wink I could tell she'd practiced a lot. "And just so you know, his name is Desmond."

We finished our sandwiches and coffee while Bethany gossiped about the other neighbors, then went to get our laundry from the dryers.

So now I knew my neighbor's name, and that he kept odd hours, drove a Jeep, and had a pretty girlfriend. Not much mystery there. But the winter jacket with the fur-lined hood was out of place and made me apprehensive. It was probably nothing, but I had to occupy my thoughts somehow.

CHAPTER 3

I woke to the sound of the most beautiful music I had ever heard coming from the hallway. It was a wind instrument, surely; having no musical talent, I had no idea what sort. At first I thought I was still asleep and dreaming, but as I got up and maneuvered myself into my chair to use the bathroom, the fog dissipated and the beautiful music persisted.

I opened my front door quietly. The music was coming from Desmond's apartment. It filled the air, rising majestically, at once somber, joyous, uplifting, and heartbreaking. I sat enraptured, unable to stop smiling, oblivious to the world—for how long I don't know—until suddenly the hall fell silent.

After a startled moment, I detected the sounds of morning traffic streaming in from the street. Light filtered through the French doors at the end of the hallway. It was just past sunrise, earlier than I typically got up.

My heart sank. I wanted the music to begin again. I sat in my doorway waiting and hoping, but the playing did not resume. Finally, I rolled back from my threshold and closed the door, fearing I might be discovered.

All day long I was haunted by the memory of what I'd heard. I recalled how much I'd feared that a musician might move in across the hall and disturb me with endless practicing or fumbling, discordant attempts at composition. But I could listen to this twenty-four hours a day and still want more. I visited Ray, to ask if he'd heard it, and if he was similarly affected. To my regret, he hadn't. He'd slept in after a wild bender with friends and drag bingo at some bar in West Hollywood. He invited me to go with him sometime. I said I'd think about it, knowing I was lying.

"If you liked the music so much, you should knock on his door and tell him," Ray suggested, mixing us Bloody Marys. "Maybe he needs a manager."

"I'm not a manager," I said. "You don't understand, Ray. Desmond should be playing in the Philharmonic. No, fuck that. He should be—"

I was cut off by the hair-raising *screech* of a car crash just outside the building. I froze, unsure of what to do with the drink in my hand. Ray was already on his way out the apartment door. I set down my drink and rolled after him into the hall and out to the fire escape, parking the cripple wagon between the open French doors and setting my emergency brake, to survey the scene.

The Villa Rosa had a clear view of one of the most dangerous intersections in LA: Fairfax and Sunset, two of Hollywood's busiest streets. Accidents happened frequently, sometimes as often as three times per week. When a crash occurred, my morbid curiosity compelled me to see how bad the damage was. The windows in both my apartment and Desmond's afforded views of the street, so I didn't need to roll out to the fire escape. But I did it anyway, because my neighbors were usually perched on the other seven fire escapes located across from or beneath mine on the top floor. We'd wave to one another or exchange comments. To me, these incidents served as sort of brief Villa Rosa social events. It was always interesting to piece together what had happened. More often than not the accidents occurred when a car headed south on Fairfax was turning east onto Sunset at a yellow light and got plowed into by someone jumping the gun on the northbound Fairfax side. Typically my neighbors and I made it out before the traffic lights had cycled again. We'd see a helpless, crying teenager or two men screaming, eager to fight. It was usually pretty clear to us who was at fault, despite not having actually witnessed the collision. I always identified with the party who got hit worst.

Sometimes the accidents were just fender benders, but this crash was a bad one. Both vehicles were crumpled. Traffic had come to a stop in all directions. Both drivers were still in their cars, and the street was strewn with shattered glass. Through the fire escape rails I saw a growing number of pedestrians gathering on Sunset to gawk. Ray, who still had his Bloody Mary, and I waited in silence for the police to arrive. They usually got there within six to ten minutes. I checked my watch, wondering how long it had taken them to reach my wreck on the freeway.

Then one of the drivers got out of her car—a girl in jeans and a blood-spattered T-shirt. She was younger than me, her movements shaky, puppet-like. Bystanders descended on her—I presumed to ensure that she was all right and didn't wander off—and quickly obscured her from view. I heard sirens approaching westbound on Sunset; their spinning lights wavered in the heat like a mirage, reminding me that Los Angeles had been built on a desert. The image of Desmond in his fur-lined parka sprang into my head. I blinked to clear it, and felt something like a warm palm on my left cheek. Instinctively I turned in that direction, and what I saw literally took my breath away.

She was only a yard from me, peering out the window of Desmond's apartment, through parted curtains, down at the chaos below us. Her eyes were large and clear, grayish with flecks of gold, wide and brimming with compassion. She had high cheekbones and a pronounced yet delicate dimpled chin, flawless, radiant pale skin, and lush, perfectly plump ruby lips that curled downward when parted. Her hair, a translucent blonde so close to white it bordered on silver, fell in soft whispers to her breasts. In short, she was heart-stoppingly beautiful, and I curse myself for not being a poet, to adequately convey it.

All this I saw in a moment, but the image remains with me to this day. I reached over and gently tapped Ray's leg, and indicated the window when he looked away from the accident. His eyes widened with awe. Then one of his cats wandered out to join us. Its eyes followed our gazes to Desmond's window. Suddenly, it went still in that way cats have when they find something to hunt, then stalked forward as if it was going to leap from the fire escape to get to that window.

"Hey!" Ray said, grabbing the cat. It struggled in his arms. "It's four stories down, dumbass," he told the Siamese as it made one last attempt to get free. Ray shifted it into a more secure hold and began petting it until it purred.

"They must have a dog or something," Ray said.

He turned his gaze back to the window where our beauty, whom I presumed to be Desmond's girlfriend, was standing. She looked at us an instant, then swiftly closed the curtains.

Bethany's remark flashed in my mind. "She stared me down like a hawk." I felt like prey.

It was a long torturous week, with many sleepless nights, before I saw her again. An insistent knock at the door across the hall brought me back to my post at the peephole, which had yet to be changed. (It was less clumsy this time, because I'd tied the phone books together after my first experiment and had them ready by the door for future need.) Looking out, I observed a delivery boy standing beside two bulging brown bags filled with groceries. He was sweating; it must have been over a hundred degrees that day. He knocked again. The door finally opened, but only as far as the security chain allowed.

"Whole Foods delivery, ma'am," the boy said. "The total is seventy-two sixty."

"My boyfriend is not here," she said softly, in an accent I could not place. "You were told to leave the bags at the door and the payment was to be handled by credit."

"Yes, ma'am," the boy responded. "But your credit card was declined, and my boss said—"

She cut him off. "Wait here," she said abruptly, then shut the door.

As the delivery boy shuffled about uneasily in the hall, I made a fast decision. Fate was offering me a chance to meet her. I got down from my perch and pushed the phone books aside, praying that she had no money in the apartment. I grabbed my wallet and keys, fixed my hair in the mirror, and waited for the perfect moment to make my entrance. I heard the chain sliding in the latch as she prepared to open her door, then quickly opened mine and rolled into the hallway just as she addressed the boy.

"I am so sorry. My boyfriend has not left me anything that I can use as payment."

I turned from locking my door, with a smile I could barely contain, and hoped I looked friendly.

"Hey there, neighbor," I said. "I couldn't help overhearing. Can I possibly help out by lending you some money? You can pay me back later."

She regarded me intently for a moment. I'd seen a similar look on people's faces before, people who had seen me in a bit part or supporting role before I'd landed my aborted big break and were trying to remember why I looked familiar. I braced myself for the look of horror and pity that usually followed when they remembered. Instead, she broke into a huge smile and seemed to look through me with the biggest, prettiest, most soulful eyes I'd ever seen.

"Thank you," she said. "I am so pleased to accept your kind offer."

I removed my wallet and paid the delivery boy with the hundred-dollar bill I kept on hand for emergencies, telling him to pocket the change. He mimed a tip of the hat to me as he accepted the bill, then turned back to her.

"Can I help you bring in the bags?"

"I'll do it," I offered. "If that's all right?" How intimidating could a man in a wheelchair be, after all, especially one who lived next door?

She smiled in agreement. The delivery boy wished us a nice day, turned on his heel, and headed down the hall and out of sight to the elevator. I scooped the overflowing bags off the floor and placed them on my lap as she opened her door wide to me.

Their apartment was a mirror image of mine, everything to the exact proportions but in reverse; the only physical difference being they had a corner window facing west down Sunset Boulevard with a view of Laurel Canyon. That they had just moved in was apparent from the many still-unopened cartons in the living room. The furniture looked like it had been purchased at IKEA, as did the cutlery and dishes spread on the folding table in their kitchen area. Articles of unlaundered male and female clothing, including underwear, lay in disorderly piles on their couch. Their Murphy bed was down, the sheets and covers unfastened and clumped together in a way that resembled a bird's nest. I felt a twinge of jealousy. Most women would have made some excuse for the mess, but it didn't seem to bother her in the slightest. I appreciated that.

"Where do you want the bags?" I asked.

"There, please," she said, indicating the kitchen counter. She studied me with a curious look that nearly made me blush as I set the bags out for her. "You can't walk," she stated flatly, as if reaching some conclusion beyond the obvious, then added, "And you are alone."

"That's me in a nutshell," I said, offering my hand. "My name's Brandon."

She paused, as if considering the correct response, then stepped forward with almost childlike energy and gave me her hand.

"My name is Kyra. It is my pleasure to meet you, Brandon."

"Likewise," I said, holding her hand gently yet firmly as I dared. Her palm felt cool against mine. Her fingers, though they appeared quite delicate, returned a pressure that seemed somehow off, as if she wasn't used to shaking hands.

"You have an interesting accent, Kyra," I said. "May I ask where you are from?"

"I do? Forgive me, I am not a native English speaker," she replied warmly, leaving my question unanswered.

I chose not to press for it. As she moved past me and attended to the groceries, I took the chance to drink in her beauty. Her hair was braided back now. No makeup (she didn't need any), and those perfect, slightly parted ruby lips. She was barefoot, taller than I'd expected, six feet at least, with a slender build. Her thin cotton dress clung loosely against her, revealing gorgeous legs with well-toned calves. Her hips were high and pronounced, her perfect breasts small and pear-shaped. She had a scent like nothing I'd ever encountered before.

"That perfume you're wearing, what is it?" I asked.

"Perfume?" she asked. "Oh, you mean how I smell?" She unabashedly sniffed her armpits, then shrugged. "That is just my smell. I am not wearing any perfume. Is it a bad smell? I am not used to such warm weather."

"Quite the opposite," I said.

She smiled and held up a carton of milk in one hand and a bag of frozen vegetables in the other. "Can you remind me which floor each one goes on?"

I assumed she meant placement in the refrigerator. How cute was that?

"The bag of vegetables goes in the freezer—top floor," I said. "The carton of milk goes on the bottom floor."

"Bag of vegetables, carton of milk," she said, placing each in its proper section of the fridge.

We played this game until all of the groceries were shelved. I could scarcely take my eyes off her. The way she laughed, the way she spoke. How curious and playful she seemed. How the fabric of her dress pulled taut against her chest when she set something high in the cupboards above her. The delicate slant of her neck and how her hair fell against it. I was mesmerized, but the attraction wasn't only physical. It was admiration of her effortless childlike quality. Besides, Desmond's belongings were everywhere: a stick of deodorant by the sink, a photograph on the refrigerator of him arm in arm with Kyra—reminders that she was the love of another man, and that I'd been reduced to less than one.

She pointed at my arms resting on the chair. "They're too big for the rest of you," she said. "Also your chest. Is it because of your chair?"

"It is," I said. "Wheeling around in this is like exercise, and I do a lot of things with my arms to make up for being unable to use my legs."

"And for vanity," she said matter-of-factly.

If anyone else had said this, I would likely have become defensive. But I found it impossible with Kyra.

"Yes," I admitted.

"Can I try it?" she asked.

"My chair?"

It took me a moment to wrap my head around this request. Yet again, there was something about Kyra's childlike curiosity that robbed the question of any possible offense.

"Why not?" I said with a laugh.

I steered close to the couch, set my brake, and did my best to shift myself out of the chair and into a normal-looking position on the couch without seeming too clumsy. Kyra came over and sat herself carefully in the chair, beaming with excitement as if I were about to teach her how to drive a racecar rather than operate a cripple wagon.

"This is a brake, which keeps me from rolling when I need to stay in place. Put your hands on the wheels—here, like this."

Within moments she was zooming around the apartment like

a child let loose at Disneyland. I taught her how to set the brakes. To do a spin. To quickly wheel back, lean back, and come forward, popping the casters and footplates off the floor into a wheelie and balance there. I never took so much delight in the delight of another, as I did watching her pump her arms against the wheel hand rims and gleefully roll around.

Suddenly the apartment door opened and in walked Desmond, in jeans and a sweat-drenched T-shirt. He was clearly taken aback by the sight of me, a strange man, sitting on his couch between piles of their dirty laundry while Kyra frolicked in a wheelchair. Then their eyes met, and some sort of communication passed between them. Desmond's scowl softened. Kyra leapt from the chair, rushed into his arms, and kissed him, molding her body to Desmond's, her fingers sliding up and into his hair. He wrapped his arms around her, holding her close. It was as if the world had fallen away and I no longer existed to them. Watching them made me ache. I wished someone could kiss me like that, like I was the only real thing in this world.

Then Desmond must have recalled I was there. He disengaged from Kyra and took me in, correctly assessing my immobility, and offered the requisite masculine dip-of-the-chin greeting.

"Desmond, come meet our neighbor across the way. His name is Brandon," Kyra said, leading him by his hand to me.

"Nice to meet you, Brandon," he said in a soft Midwestern accent, and powerfully grasped my hand. I'd expected him to speak in a deeper version of Kyra's strange accent, and his Roman nose and dark coloring had led me to think he might be Italian. I found myself intrigued ... and oddly disappointed.

"The boy came with our groceries," Kyra told Desmond. "There was a problem with the payment card, so Brandon paid him for us. He helped me put everything away."

"That was awful kind of you," Desmond said. "Tell me how much it was, and I'll pick up some cash this evening and drop it by, if that's all right?"

His voice was courteous and friendly, his manner polite. His eyes told me that despite me being a cripple who could offer him no competition for Kyra's affections, he saw me as a threat. I was almost flattered.

"It was seventy-two sixty," I said, omitting the tip as my guilty pleasure. Kyra pushed the wheelchair to where I was sitting on the couch. I managed myself into it, feeling self-conscious and out of place as she rejoined Desmond and once more took his hand.

"I've got to get going. I have plans with friends this afternoon," I lied. From the way they were staring at each other, I was unsure if they heard me.

After a long, uncomfortable pause, Desmond looked down at me.

"Sure, Brandon," he said casually. "Thanks again. Really nice to meet you. I hope Kyra didn't say anything that freaked you out. She can sound a bit off if she forgets to take her medication."

His words affected me like a bowl of ice water poured over my head. Was Kyra's "otherness," her endearing, childlike quality, in fact some emotional or mental issue to be medicated into normalcy?

Kyra seemed displeased by Desmond's remarks. She frowned at him when he said that, then swished away toward the bathroom.

"She was absolutely lovely," I said. "I'll let myself out."

As I inserted the key in my lock, I heard Desmond bolt his door behind me.

I spent the remainder of the day helplessly reliving my encounter with Kyra moment by moment; it took a sleeping pill to eventually knock me out.

A long, deep moan pulled me out of a dreamless sleep. It seemed to be

coming from someplace nearby. Throwing off the covers, I got out of bed. Another masculine moan, a simultaneous gasp of feminine pleasure. I had no doubt Desmond and Kyra were making love in their Murphy bed. Their sounds drew me to my door in voyeuristic curiosity and mounting jealousy. I found my door open, as was theirs across the hall. Kyra's voice called my name, beckoning me to join them. Though the distance was only a few feet, it took me over a hundred steps to reach their apartment. As I walked in, I saw them: Kyra naked astride Desmond on their bed, sweating, her back and neck arched as she undulated her hips, nipples hard and breasts swollen as they rocked skyward, eyes glazed and lips parted, gasping as she writhed against him. Desmond gripped her legs, his eyes transfixed upon Kyra's heaving chest. Suddenly the two of them turned in unison to regard me, each raising a hand to motion me to the bed as they continued grinding their bodies together. Nervous, shamed by my intrusion yet unable to resist the invitation to come closer, I moved to them. They reached over to clasp my hands, their twin grips tightening against each hand painfully until I could barely distinguish their hands from my own. Kyra moved faster and faster on Desmond's lap, emitting guttural sounds like bird cries yet strangely beautiful. The song pierced my heart. Her cries grew louder, faster, finally reaching a peak as Kyra and Desmond contorted in climax.

They released my hands and fell against each other. Kyra was crying. Desmond turned to me with a satisfied smile.

"I break her heart with love," he said.

My eyes shot open. I stared into the silent darkness surrounding my bed.

The next morning there was an envelope under my door, with *Thank You* written across it and seventy-three dollars inside. I had the sneaking suspicion *Thank You* really meant "Fuck you, stay away from my girlfriend." I couldn't blame Desmond. He'd seen the way I looked at Kyra. I considered myself lucky to have spent that time with her, brief though it had been. I realized that

I hardly knew any more about them now than I had before. Who they were, where they came from, how they'd met, what either of them did for a living—these remained mysteries.

That afternoon I saw Desmond leave, and soon afterward I went to knock on their door. Kyra opened it, but left the security chain in place.

"Hello, Brandon," she said, with a sadness in her eyes that broke my heart.

"Hey, Kyra," I said, trying to sound upbeat. "I was wondering if you and Desmond had plans for tonight?"

She looked through me in that way that she could and shook her head.

"I am so sorry, Brandon. I like you, but Desmond does not think we should be friends. We move around a lot, and he has a silly fear of me getting attached to people."

"But—"

"I am so sorry," she repeated, and closed the door.

Devastated, I rolled back to my apartment. No sooner was I inside than the beautiful music began again. Her music, I realized now. Only now it was no longer somber and majestic. It was tortured, and wrenched my insides. I sat at my kitchen table, poured myself a glass of wine from an open bottle, and took a swig. It had gone bitter, but I swallowed it anyway. I lay my head on the cold Formica as Kyra played on and I wept—huge, heaving sobs escaping my useless body in violent, uncontrollable spasms.

CHAPTER 4

I slept through most of the next week. When I was awake, I drank myself into oblivion with my four new friends, whose names all curiously began with the letter J: Johnny W., Jim B., Jack D., and Jose C. We scoffed at the thought of mixers.

Late one night—it must have been after two—I heard a soft knock at my door. I opened it, fully expecting to see Ray or Bethany standing there, as occasionally happened. Some deranged, besotted part of me hoped it might be Kyra. Instead, I beheld two odd, somewhat bent strangers: an elderly, gaunt, balding man in a dark suit and tie, and, behind him, a heavyset woman I guessed to be in her sixties, wearing an ill-fitting gown and large dark glasses, her chubby hands gripping a cane. Before I had a chance to ask who they were, the old man tentatively addressed me.

"We spoke on the phone? My name is Arthur. This is Mrs. Tremaine. I do hope we're not too early, Desmond."

The door across the hall opened.

"No, this way. I'm Desmond."

The man turned his head, then glanced nervously back at me.

"My apologies for disturbing you," he said.

He turned again, placed a practiced hand on the heavyset woman's arm, and steered her across the hall into the apartment. I realized she must be blind. Desmond gave me his chin dip, as if encountering each other like this in the middle of the night was completely normal and he hadn't ruthlessly cut me out of his and Kyra's lives. Then he entered his apartment after the couple and closed the door.

I was intoxicated, so my mind was moving slowly, but inevitably questions began to form. Who were those old people? And what business did they have with Desmond at this ungodly hour?

I wheeled out to the fire escape, hoping that I might be able to see what was going on inside their apartment. But their curtains were drawn. It was time for another session at the peephole. Even if I had to sit there all night, I would see what happened when the old couple left the apartment.

I rolled back to my studio, poured myself a tall Jack D. on ice, and took up my post, nursing my drink while I waited. Did I imagine that I heard sounds coming from across the hall, the men's voices raised in argument? Later (I was close to the bottom of my glass, I admit), I was sure I heard Kyra moaning with pleasure. I pictured her as I'd seen her in my dream, conjuring the old couple admiring Kyra and Desmond writhing naked before them on the bed. Would the sounds of lovemaking be enough for the blind woman? I pictured Desmond and Kyra reaching out, their nubile flesh connecting with wrinkled skin as Kyra made that haunting, birdlike cry in climax. Then ...

Silence.

I sat digesting these disturbing products of my obsessed imagination.

I snapped to when the apartment door opened and the old couple appeared. The man was calm, as if nothing unusual had transpired. The woman seemed agitated. The door closed, and he guided her out of my line of vision. I listened to her cane *tap-*

tapping as they made their way slowly down the hall to the elevator.

I wheeled myself to my window in time to witness them emerge, arm in arm, from the front of the Villa Rosa, get into a waiting limousine, and drive west along Sunset.

What on Earth had just taken place across the hall? I was certain I'd heard something, and it sure as hell sounded like sex. Was screwing for voyeurs how Desmond and Kyra made a living? He rarely left the building for more than an hour, and as far as I could tell she never left it at all.

That afternoon I asked Bethany about it as we sat drinking Jack D. and Cokes, waiting for our clothes to dry.

"Whatever they're doing up there, I'll bet it's illegal," she said. "Maybe they're porn stars, and the oldsters are producers. I bet people would happily pay to watch them screw. Wouldn't you? I know I would."

I was saved from having to respond by Ray appearing just then behind me.

"There you are, Bethany. It's time to get ready for bingo," he said. "We want to get there before the mobs arrive."

He looked like he'd dropped in from the 1980s, from that Olivia Newton-John video "Physical": tight yellow satin shorts, orange knee-high socks, and a hot pink, low-cut T-shirt. He seemed excited. "You come, too, Brandon. I'm driving. You know you want to."

The fact was I'd politely refused Ray on countless Wednesdays before this.

"Do join us, Brandon," Bethany chimed in, catching Ray's enthusiasm. "It sounds like fun."

"C'mon, Brandon. Don't be a stick-in-the-mud. There may be celebrity guests."

"The last thing I want to see."

"I'll pay your twenty-dollar game fee. It all goes to charity."

Still I hesitated. Sensing that I was possibly wavering, Ray applied the *coup de grâce*.

"Drinks are half price."

That clinched it.

"Fuck it," I said. "Why not? I haven't left this building in over a month. Let's do it."

I'd try anything to get my mind off Kyra and Desmond—even play bingo with drag queens.

"Hooray!" said Bethany.

"Good," Ray added, clearly delighted. "That just leaves a little matter of appropriate garb. You can't go looking like that."

"I'm sure I don't own anything that could pass for what you have in mind."

"I'll take care of it," Bethany offered.

"I'm not dressing in drag," I protested.

"We won't have to go that far. But first we need to get our things from the dryers. Meet Ray and me at my apartment at five o'clock."

So there I sat in Bethany's bathroom, in the midst of every imaginable feminine product, while Bethany applied mascara to my eyelashes, rouge to my cheeks, and gel to my hair. Ray contributed a T-shirt with the word FABULOUS in rhinestones across the chest, along with a feather boa. I wore both to prove that I could. Looking at myself in the mirror, I assumed Tim Curry's character in *The Rocky Horror Picture Show*. Bethany switched tops unabashedly in front of us, revealing pierced nipples and a navel ring as she buttoned into a tight leather vest with long, gaudy beaded fringes. I brought along the HANDI-CAPPED placard I'd been issued, in the event that we had trouble with parking.

Gladys was watering irises in the courtyard; she greeted each of us by name, not batting an eyelash at our outlandish appearance. Bethany and I chatted with her about the weather—wasn't it nice out today, for a change?—while Ray went to fetch his

Volkswagen. After I'd maneuvered myself into the passenger seat, he folded my cripple wagon into the hatchback. As we headed down Santa Monica Boulevard in West Hollywood, we sang along at the top of our lungs with 1980s selections from Ray's iTunes.

We left the car in the International House of Pancakes parking lot on Santa Monica near La Cienega Boulevard. It's free, whereas the side streets are all permit only. Then we made our way the four blocks back to the corner of Sweetzer.

Hamburger Mary's was already packed with patrons from the festive air-conditioned interior to the raucous outdoor patio. I had never seen so many men dressed like women. Some of them were quite pretty. Besides the waiters, all in garish finery, there were a lot of obviously gay men strutting their well-toned, often shirtless bodies, and openly fondling or making out with other men. I prided myself that it did not disturb me in the slightest. One table looked like it might be a family, complete with a grandmother and teenage kids. Most of the straight people present were couples. Ray pointed them out to Bethany and me; they congregated in the back, broadcasting that they were together by holding hands. Like everyone else, they appeared to be having a grand time, happy to follow the advice in lights above the bar: EAT. DRINK. AND BE ... MARY.

We sat by the edge of the stage, a raised platform with a large mirrored disco ball beside the bingo board backed by lurid gold drapes, with a large pipe extending from the ceiling to the floor, and a table covered with equally outré fabric. At seven o'clock, a slim guy with short, gray-blond hair wearing faded jeans and a "Bingo Boy" T-shirt began the proceedings with a big smile, welcoming the crowd and asking, "What's the name of the game?"

To which almost everyone present—including Ray—shouted, "BINGO!"

"How do we play it?"

"LOUDLY!"

Obviously there were a lot of regulars.

Ray told us the emcee had been a successful AIDS fundraiser in the Eighties before founding the bingo games at Hamburger Mary's in 1998. After quipping with the audience, Bingo Boy turned things over to the numbers caller, the tallest, ugliest, hairiest transvestite I'd ever seen. He sat at the table turning a plastic globe on a spit, causing the yellow balls faced with black letters and numbers to bounce wildly.

"B-9," he announced, flashing his eyes and adding flamboyantly, "That's a vitamin we all need to maintain our sex drive!"

Everyone laughed. Clearly this was not going to be like the bingo played in church basements.

The twenty-dollar entrance fee had got each player ten bingo sheets and one grand prize card. Bethany, Ray, and I shared a pitcher of margaritas. As the games proceeded, Bethany and I learned that each round had a different name. There was a "Frank and Beans" round and a "Rim Job" round, and rules for what constituted a win changed from game to game. Sometimes the numbers had to all be vertical or horizontal, or only in corners. Other times it was regular bingo, with diagonals allowed. So you had to pay attention. The "Blackout" round required that every square on your card be filled.

During one game, Bethany called a false bingo and had to go onto the stage amid cheerful jeers from the crowd, to be spanked by the caller with a paddle. Real winners were pelted by the losers with their balled-up non-winning bingo sheets as they made their way to the stage to claim their prizes. If more than one player called "Bingo!" all of them went up and picked one unseen ball apiece out of a bag. The highest number won; the rest got booby prizes they fished out of another bag. All of the winners' prizes, donated by the charity benefited that evening, were good—champagne baskets, brunch certificates—and always included lube. The grand prize at the end included gift cards (for a free haircut at two separate salons, a sixty-minute massage, the Coffee Bean, Sprinkles Cupcakes, and Trader Joe's, and for

Indian, Thai, and Italian food); assorted teas, chocolate, biscuits, spices, and seasonings from local specialty shops; a beautiful blanket; and five seasons of a hit cable TV series on DVD.

When certain numbers were called, all the audience regulars would shout responses. "I-22" produced "Quack, quack!" (Because, Ray explained, if you've had enough to drink 22 looks like swimming ducks). "B-11" was "Legs to Heaven!" and "G-54" evoked "The Disco G" (for the former disco Studio 54), often accompanied by "Woo-woo!" Any letter with "69" was greeted with cheers and catcalls.

At one point the caller looked down at me with a lewd smile.

"You—Mr. Fabulous. Quit looking up my dress!"

"I swear I wasn't," I said, raising my hands with innocent submission.

"Then maybe you should start, honey!"

And he exposed his penis, provoking a huge burst of laughter from the crowd. Bethany literally spat out her drink, spraying me. I didn't mind.

The drinks poured liberally. Between games everyone sang 1980s hits. During one break the hairy drag queen plopped himself onto my lap.

"Don't worry, honey," he whispered in my ear, his breath stinking of cigarettes. "I know you're straight, but I've got a thing for handsome men in wheelchairs. They can't run away from me. Let me stay for just a little while."

By the end of the first session, we were on our third pitcher of margaritas. We decided to stay for the second, which began at nine. The house bought us all shots of something sweet and fragrant. We were beyond inebriated, but Ray ordered a fourth pitcher anyway. By midnight the second session had ended. The grand prize included Ray-Ban sunglasses, a $100 gift certificate to Apple, a bottle of Grey Goose vodka, DVDs, and lots more. And we were still drinking. I'd lost count of how many I'd had, and didn't care.

Bethany insisted that we eat something. I had a burger

stuffed with gooey cheese. Ray ordered a Sloppy Mary (open-faced and smothered in chili and cheeses). Bethany ordered mac-and-cheese balls and deep-fried pickles. I noticed her attention was repeatedly drawn to an attractive young straight couple making out in the back.

"What's up?" I asked.

"He's one of my regulars," she said. "I'm guessing that's his wife or girlfriend. I'm not jealous or anything, it's just that he stiffed me the last time we hung out, and he's been dodging my calls."

I glowered in his direction.

"Don't worry about it," Bethany said, tussling my hair. "I'm fine."

"I want to worry about it," I said. I motioned to our waiter, another hairy transvestite in heavy war paint. "Can you please total our check and deliver it to that guy over there?" I indicated Bethany's client. "He's paying."

We watched the confused look on the guy's face when the waiter delivered the bill and pointed to us. Cornered, Scumbag could do nothing but wave to Bethany. I couldn't imagine what he would tell his wife or girlfriend to explain what had just happened. Too bad for him.

I kept my eye on Scumbag, expecting a confrontation, and I was right. When his lady friend went to the powder room, he headed to our table. I was ready for him.

"What the fuck, Bethany?" he said. "You trying to out me in front of my wife?"

I turned sharply and rolled onto his foot, braking hard and pressing the wheel down with all the strength of my left hand while reaching out to clutch his balls with my right. Suffice it to say he was pinned, and I had his full attention.

"Listen to me, Scumbag," I said. "You owe my friend money. Just pay the bill and walk away." I gave him a firm squeeze. "And don't forget to leave a nice tip, or you'll hear from me again."

I released my hold on his nuts as his wife passed near our table and gave us an inquisitive look.

"Keep an eye on him, honey child," I called out to her. "He's one handsome, irascible devil."

Bethany, Ray, and I watched with delight as he went back to his table, motioned the waiter over, paid both bills, and hastily ushered his spouse out of the club.

"My hero," Bethany said, beaming brightly and clapping her hands. Ray joined her in applauding my performance. I acknowledged them with a mock bow. How fortunate I'd been to find my way to the Villa Rosa. Where else could a transvestite, an escort, and a cripple feel at home together, without fear of judgment?

We straggled out of Hamburger Mary's shortly after two, three of the last celebrants to depart. Bethany was too drunk even to walk. She sat in my lap with her arms around my neck as I wheeled us out of the bar. Her weight against my torso and her half-conscious embrace were the first real physical contact I'd had in a long time. I let myself enjoy it. When we reached Ray's car, I told him he was too drunk to drive. He insisted that he could.

"Look at me, Ray," I said. "I'm in this wheelchair because some schmuck as drunk as we are now decided he could drive. Now my life is shit, and he's dead. Let's live to play another day, all right? Leave the car. It's fine with my placard. I'll call us a cab."

He couldn't argue with that.

The cab driver went up La Cienega, but instead of turning onto Fountain Avenue to avoid traffic he went forward another block to Sunset, a bad idea at closing time. Almost the first thing I saw as we headed east to the Villa Rosa was the well-lit billboard for the series I'd been set to star in. It was about twelve stories high, covering the side of the Andaz Hotel. My mood immediately crashed. We moved at a crawl. Bethany was out cold with her head on my shoulder, wedged between Ray and me. Ray was lost in his thoughts. I watched the slowly passing sights on the strip, inwardly cursing the driver for taking this infernal route. Young people in expensive evening wear stumbled out of the clubs on healthy legs, lighting cigarettes and saying goodbyes. Some would continue their debauchery at a VIP after party, where anyone who hadn't hooked up yet still had a chance. They had no idea how lucky they all were.

It was almost three in the morning when the cab finally pulled up outside the Villa Rosa. It had taken us nearly forty minutes to travel about fifteen blocks. The first thing I noticed was the old couple getting into the limousine. They'd come to see Kyra and Desmond again, and I'd missed them. I hurried the driver to remove my wheelchair from the trunk. As I attempted drunkenly to maneuver out of the cab and into it, I failed to set the brake and the wheelchair rolled away. I fell hard against the curb. More embarrassed than hurt, I struggled to regain my dignity and lift myself, shrugging the driver away as he tried to help me. He stepped backward, pity in his eyes.

"Bring my chair over, *please*," I said through gritted teeth.

Ray and Bethany joined me as he complied. "You're bleeding, Brandon," Bethany said.

I looked down. I'd gouged both my elbows on the curb. I could also taste blood in my mouth. I ran my tongue over my lower lip; I'd cut that as well. Too embarrassed to accept help, and too drunk to realize I needed it, I told Bethany and Ray to go on ahead of me. They reluctantly agreed then slouched toward the building, so wasted they had to hold each other up.

I paid the driver with a credit card, then wheeled myself over to the entrance and punched in my code. As the buzzer sounded, opening the security gate, I looked up at Kyra's windows.

There she was, nude, peering straight down at me—or rather through me. I might as well have been naked myself, stripped as I felt of all my pride. Time stopped as I gazed at her. The soft ceiling light gave her nearly translucent hair a halolike effect; her thin body was enveloped by shadows. My vision swam. My heart pounded in my chest. Then Desmond appeared at the window beside her, closed the curtains, and put out the light.

I found Bethany sitting on the floor outside my apartment door, knees drawn up beneath her chin, arms clutched around her legs.

"Ray's gone to bed," she said. "Would it be okay if I came in with you?"

I sensed that she needed it to be, though I was wary of her expectations.

"Sure," I said.

Once inside, I rolled to the bathroom, washed the cuts on my elbows, and covered them with Band-Aids. Bethany wanted another drink, and so did I after seeing Kyra. We each had a shot from one of my bottles. At some point Bethany asked if she could stay for what remained of the night.

"I don't want to be alone," she explained. "But I don't want to have sex, if that's all right?"

I told her she was welcome, and that I couldn't have sex even if she did want to.

She lowered my Murphy bed, and we got into it together. She began to speak softly, in a voice different from her usual coarse language, telling me things about her past that made me understand her current situation a lot better. When she was a child, a family friend had repeatedly molested her. The abuse was so severe it left her unable to have children (not that she wanted any). Sex gave her no pleasure and never had; it was just a way to pay the bills until she completed school and earned her degree. She hoped and prayed that someday she could stop selling her body and find someone who really loved her.

She sobbed quietly against my chest. I thought about how both of us had been brutally robbed of our sexuality. And then I whispered my own darkest fear to her, that I had never told anyone: that I might not be entirely blameless for my condition. I'm not sure if she heard me.

We lay silent in the dark for a while. Then Bethany shifted

her body away from mine and snuggled back against me with a pressure that in days gone by I would have taken as a signal to initiate sex. But that wasn't what this was about. I wrapped one arm around her, across her shoulders and upper chest, and cuddled her protectively. She took my hand and pressed it softly against her breasts. We fell asleep like that; just two human beings comforting each other, sharing their warmth with no expectations and nothing to prove.

CHAPTER 5

I woke up alone, hungover, and miserable, with a sense of futility regarding my future I had not felt before. Bethany was gone. No doubt she was as embarrassed by what she'd revealed to me as I was by what I'd revealed to her, and didn't want to face me. I lay in bed until well after noon brooding, lamenting my lost career and my current lack of prospects. I considered taking a sleeping pill to knock myself out, but decided against it. My elbows stung down to the bones; my lip felt swollen. Nausea forced me to get up.

As I raised myself to the chair, I felt dizzy and ready to vomit. The vertigo grew worse as I wheeled myself quickly toward the bathroom. I barely made it to the toilet, where noxious fluids streamed out of me from every possible orifice.

I took a long look in the bathroom mirror. Remnants of smeared makeup surrounded my eyes. The word FABULOUS still glittered on the disheveled T-shirt I'd fallen asleep in. Suffice it to say that was the opposite of how I was feeling.

A shower and clean clothes only helped a little. I spent the rest of the afternoon on my couch watching senseless talk shows on which this one slept with that one's stepsister, or that one denied fathering this one's child. The truth of the matter resided in an envelope the host waved high overhead like a threat before opening it to reveal what was already obvious to anyone with eyes. I couldn't shake the thought that life was senseless—or, worse yet, not worth living. To add insult to injury, during station breaks the network ran continuous ads for the pilot of the series I had been cast in before the accident. The premiere was airing that night. Rather than just turn the damn TV off and seek out something to distract me—like maybe drop in on Ray—I determined that I would watch the show.

I whiled away the hours with my new German friend, Jäger M., replaying all the sorry events of my life. Then I sat stone-faced while the young actor who replaced me butchered the opening scene. When the credits appeared and my name wasn't among them, I switched off the set, unable to bear watching another second. But I hadn't tortured myself enough yet. I went online to see if I could find out anything about Felicia. I found something, all right: a picture of my former girlfriend arm in arm with the guy from her acting class, on a red carpet attending some movie premiere. Her career was thriving, and so, apparently, was her love life. If there was a God, what clearer signs could He offer that He hated me?

But I didn't have to keep suffering, I decided. I'd show Him. And I'd make it dramatic, too.

I rolled down the hall to the stairway to the roof, and set my brake at the bottom step. There were thirteen steps in all. I maneuvered myself into a seated position on the second step then used my hands to inch my ass backward from step to step upward, until I reached the heavy fire door. I pushed it open. The balmy night air *whooshed* against me. I dragged myself across grainy, soot-covered shingles, past airshafts and cable wires, between several satellite dishes, until I reached the front of the building.

The ledge was about two feet high. With effort, I pulled myself onto it, rotated my hips so my legs swung over the edge, and balanced there, taking in the spectacle. Bethany had once informed me the roof offered great views of the city, and she was right. Ahead of me the green hills of Laurel Canyon erupted skyward, dotted with multimillion-dollar homes. The HOLLY-WOOD sign loomed over Beachwood Canyon in the east like a slug line establishing the location. Of course, God added a twisted joke just for me: the panorama included the billboard for my television show. I gave Him the laugh.

Perhaps fifteen feet below me jutted my fire escape, with Sunset Boulevard sprawled four stories down, speckled with white headlights and red taillights moving slowly all the way toward the heart of Hollywood in the east, and westward to where the boulevard ended at the breathtaking expanse of the Pacific Ocean.

I looked down at the hard cement, and there once again was the familiar limousine for the third night in a row. I watched the old man help the woman out of the backseat. If I repositioned myself right, I might be able to hit the limo; all it required was the slightest shift of balance. My ego was just drunk enough to do it, and my heart was just sober enough to consent. Wouldn't that give them something to chat about with Desmond and Kyra before their next session? The woman assembled her cane and *tap-tapped* her way toward the front gate with her companion's arm for support.

What the hell were the four of them doing together? It would be nice to solve the mystery before I shuffled off this mortal coil. Suddenly I recalled Bethany's guess—that Kyra and Desmond might be porn stars. If that were the case, they would likely show up somewhere online.

Legs dangling from the roof edge, I carefully withdrew my phone from my pocket. I didn't know their surnames, but hoped their first names together might be enough. I brought up a browser and searched "Desmond and Kyra" a half dozen ways, including Facebook, Twitter, Snapchat, Instagram, and even several porn sites. I found nothing of relevance. No photos that remotely resembled either of them. If those were their real names, their porn names would be different, but there should be something. It was rare for people to manage to hide from the net these days. They had to turn up somewhere, if only I found the right subjects to match against one or both of them. I tried "Kyra porn star" and "Kyra sex slave." Nothing, at least not that related to my Kyra. Then "Kyra model" and "Kyra actress." Lots of hits for those, but not the Kyra I sought. I tried "Kyra Villa Rosa," "Kyra beauty queen," and "Kyra love." No dice. I just didn't have enough data.

Maybe I could find something about the old couple. What were their names? I pictured my first encounter with them. What had the man called himself? Arthur! And the woman was Mrs. Tremaine. That was quite possibly searchable. I typed "Tremaine Blindness" and had her in seconds.

Margaret Tremaine was an agent at one of the more prestigious agencies in town, with several clients whose names I recognized. She had adult onset diabetes with complications that led to blindness. One of her clients praised her enthusiasm and creative input as key factors to his success, in an interview on Salon.com. *Variety* and *The Hollywood Reporter* had articles about film deals she'd negotiated with all the major studios. There were photos of her before she went blind, toned, healthy, smiling alongside famous celebrities at red carpet events like the Oscars. She looked happy, her blue eyes beaming. How much weight she had gained, and how feeble she seemed now! Compassion welled in me for her, regardless of whatever she and Arthur were up to with Kyra and Desmond.

Suddenly Margaret Tremaine herself stepped onto the fire escape below me—alone—and gripped the railing. Her face glowed in the moonlight. No longer wearing her dark glasses, she was clearly staring out at the street. She lifted her hands and gazed at them in wonder, a beatific smile on her face. Three nights ago Mrs. Tremaine had walked into the Villa Rosa blind. She was still blind when I saw her below a short while ago. Now she could see again.

I sat stunned for several minutes after she retreated from the fire escape, wondering if I was so drunk I was seeing things that weren't there. I was reassured when I observed Arthur exiting the front gate below me followed by Mrs. Tremaine, no longer using her cane. As the limousine drove out of sight, it seemed to take the dark clouds that hung over me along with it.

I realized that I had witnessed a miracle—and that I would have missed it by mere minutes had I done what I was contemplating and jumped. My mind reeled. I was convinced that whatever had transpired between Mrs. Tremaine and my neighbors was responsible for the transformation. It couldn't possibly be a coincidence that the cure occurred just when Arthur and Mrs. Tremaine happened to be visiting the Villa Rosa. Were Desmond and Kyra some sort of healers? Could those unopened cartons contain wonder-working herbs they'd smuggled in from whatever country Kyra hailed from? Or was something supernatural at work? I didn't see how it could have been accomplished, nor did I really care at that moment. Something inside me, some long suppressed element of childlike wonder, welled up and erupted, assuring me that if sight could be returned to the blind, mobility could be restored to the lame. Desmond had exiled me from their lives, but nothing would keep me from them if he and Kyra could heal me. I wanted it, and I would do whatever it took to convince them to do for me what they had done for Mrs. Tremaine.

Filled with renewed purpose, I lifted my legs carefully, one at a time, back over the edge, lowered myself to the roof, crawled across the gritty shingles to the door, and pulled myself inside. I *thump-thumped* down the thirteen steps, barely able to contain my excitement. I was even grateful to see my wheelchair waiting on the fourth-floor landing as I'd left it. Virtually leaping astride it, I quickly rolled myself down the hallway to Desmond and Kyra's door.

Now that I was there, what would I say to them? That I had seen Mrs. Tremaine leave the building, knew that she was no longer blind, and would they please cure me? Wouldn't I sound crazy? Was I, after all? It was late. But who could blame me for ignoring the hour in light of what had occurred? I reached to knock, then paused. What if they denied having helped Mrs. Tremaine?

I knocked. No response. I let several moments pass and knocked again, louder this time. Still no response. Were they deliberately not answering, knowing it was me at the door? I pictured them sitting on their couch stifling giggles. Gripped with anxiety, I gave the door a solid pounding. Still nothing. I placed my ear to the wood and listened for over a minute, but heard no stirring. I banged several more times, surprised that I didn't wake any of the other tenants.

Finally I gave up. Desmond and Kyra must have gone out. I rolled across the hall to my apartment, assuring myself that I'd see them soon and somehow convince them to help me. They had to; I had no other options.

I couldn't sleep for the few hours that remained of the night. When I knocked on their door in the morning, I again got no response. I assumed they must still be asleep. Anxious and hungry, I forced myself to go and eat some breakfast at the Griddle, a popular café down the block on Sunset.

Gladys was busily at work in the courtyard when I rolled back into the Villa Rosa about a half hour later, carrying an assortment of muffins I planned to offer my neighbors along with my plea for salvation. During a brief interchange about some proposed building upgrades, she mentioned that Desmond had notified the building manager he'd be moving out by the last day of the month, and had forfeited the rent deposit due to the short notice. I immediately excused myself and took a fast roll around the block, circling it twice then riding along each side street, searching for Desmond's Jeep. It was nowhere in sight.

When there was still no answer at their apartment, I went into mine and wrote a note including my cell phone number:

PLEASE CALL ME. IT'S URGENT. BRANDON.

I taped it from their door to the doorframe in such a way that it would be clear if it were moved, then retired to my apartment to wait, beside myself with worry. The end of the month was five days away. I feared I would never see Kyra and Desmond again.

I lost track of time. Finally there came a knock. They'd returned and seen my note! My heart leapt. I sped to open the door.

My disappointment must have registered on my face when I discovered, not Desmond or Kyra, but Father Tom, a young priest from my family's parish. Too young and too handsome to be a priest in this town, I'd often thought, as did many of his followers, I suspected.

"I'm not here to trouble you, Brandon," he greeted me defensively. "May I come in and speak with you for a moment?"

I reluctantly let him in, observing my note across the hall just as I'd left it.

Father Tom looked dour in black jeans, black shoes and socks, and a black shirt with his requisite stiff white priest's collar. I followed his gaze as he stared around my apartment, taking in the general messiness, the closed blinds, the scattered empty liquor bottles.

"Your mother is concerned about your safety, Brandon," he began. "She asked me to visit you, to see how you're doing. One of your neighbors happened to be leaving the building when I arrived, and was kind enough to let me in. It appears that you've been keeping yourself busy. And I can't help adding that you haven't been to church once since your accident."

"God and I aren't on the best of terms lately, Father," I said, trying not to show how apprehensive I was at his being there.

Father Tom proceeded to perform his priestly duty.

"You feel like He's no longer standing beside you," he said.

"And you're right. But it's not because God has abandoned you, Brandon. It's because He's been carrying you."

"That's very Hallmark card of you, Father," I said. "I appreciate you coming by, but I'm fine. I promise."

"Your mother tells me you haven't taken her calls for months now. What's up with that, Brandon?"

The younger members of the congregation loved Father Tom for his plain street talk.

"You know how my mom can get, Father. I don't blame her. I suppose I have been wallowing a bit in self-pity. I'm feeling a lot more hopeful now. Honest to God."

He pulled open my curtains to let in the noonday sun, then seated himself on my couch.

"To what do we owe this newfound hope?" he asked.

He'd always been great at tossing the ball in my court, but I couldn't just tell him the truth regarding my aspirations with the neighbors across the hall, could I? He might think I was crazy to believe what I did, which was ironic if you thought about it. Or maybe he actually had information, secret information only priests knew, that could help me. Unsure how best to proceed, I decided to throw the ball back in his court to test the waters.

"Have you ever witnessed a miracle, Father? A real miracle?"

He paused before he answered, no doubt to show that he took me seriously.

"I guess that depends on what you consider a real miracle."

"Have you ever seen someone miraculously healed? A blind person granted sight? A crippled person get up and walk?"

"To be honest, I haven't. But I have seen patients with cancer suddenly enter remission and make full recoveries, through what I believe is the power of prayer."

"What would you do if you did?" I persisted.

"If I saw someone miraculously healed?"

"Yes."

I could see that I'd made him uncomfortable. He had to be thinking that I was talking about my own paralysis and hoping that I could be cured. It must be common for people he coun-seled in my situation.

"As a priest, I'd need evidence that that was indeed what I'd witnessed," he said after a pause. "I suppose, like anyone, I'd investigate the cause of the injury and results of the healing for confirmation. But I'd keep firmly in mind that God has His reasons for allowing some people to be sick and others to be healed. I believe everything happens in accordance with His plan for each of us. He may need you in that wheelchair for some purpose you may never fully understand. If it is His will for you to walk again, rest assured that nothing will stand in His way until you do. My advice is to take a breather, Brandon. Surrender to His will and see how that goes for you. The world may surprise you."

Father Tom was a good man, but it was clear I'd be taking a risk if I told him I'd found a way to walk again that likely didn't include God. Sermon delivered, he got up and placed his hands on my shoulders. I submitted without protest, unexpectedly soothed and inspired by his visit—yet eager for him to leave.

"Call your mother, Brandon," he said. "And maybe take it a bit easier on the drinking."

He handed me his card and invited me to call or text him at any time, day or night, for guidance or a friendly ear. I thanked him and said I would, and let him out the door. His confession that he, himself, would feel obligated to "investigate the cause of the injury and results of the healing for confirmation" had given me all the ecclesiastical permission I needed to spring into action before it was too late.

CHAPTER 6

*T*he cab deposited me in front of the Creative Artists Agency's block-long building on the grandiosely named Avenue of the Stars in Century City. CAA is one of the top talent brokers in the world. If actors were like prostitutes, CAA was their proud madam. Having CAA represent you in the shark-infested Hollywood waters means that your talents are well worth exploiting—that is, until you burn out. CAA is so exclusive, it's almost impossible even to get beyond the reception area into the actual offices. The building's planners wanted to impress insiders and intimidate everyone else; once upon a time it would have impressed me, but no longer.

CAA was not my agency, so I had no reason to expect a welcome as I wheeled myself into the vast marble-and-glass lobby. It took almost a minute to get to the monumental grand marble staircase and past it down the wide hall to the long white-and-black marble CAA reception counter. Behind panes of glass, six attractive, perfectly groomed young women with earpieces answered phones like automatons.

"CAA, how may I direct your call?"

Seeing me approach, one of them swished her ponytail and smiled.

"Welcome to CAA, how can I help you?" she asked.

"I'm here to see Margaret Tremaine," I said, offering the most disarming smile I could muster.

"Do you have an appointment?"

I lied without blinking, then gave her my name when she asked for it. Her ponytail bobbed as she put through a call and received instructions.

"I'm sorry, there must be some confusion. Mrs. Tremaine isn't in today, and your name isn't in her calendar. Her assistant requests that you please call to reschedule."

I was prepared for the block.

"And I'm sorry to hear that Mrs. Tremaine isn't in the office. She asked me to come down today, and I've gone to great lengths to accommodate her." I glanced down at my wheelchair. "If it's not too much trouble, may I talk to her assistant? Say I work for *The Hollywood Reporter*."

"Just a moment," the receptionist said, smiling sweetly at me.

Clearly the situation was above her pay grade and required a more delicate brush-off than she was in a position to deliver. She dipped her head, speaking low enough to conceal the ensuing conversation, which anyway I couldn't observe from the vantage point of my wheelchair.

"Someone will be right down," she informed me. "Please wait over there. Can I offer you a beverage?"

"No, thank you," I said, and wheeled myself to the alcove she'd indicated.

In clear view of the reception counter, the waiting area consisted of four pairs of bulky, dark leather armchairs perpendicular to the wall in two groupings, with two low, solid cubes separating each pair of facing twin chairs. Atop each cube was a colorful potted orchid, to contrast with the slick white marble surface, with that day's editions of *The Hollywood Reporter* and *Variety* and other industry periodicals as further accents. The designer obviously hadn't planned space for wheelchairs, so I set my brake at a ninety-degree angle to one of the cubes, and pretended to occupy myself with a magazine while I waited, trying not to feel additionally self-conscious about sticking out and ruining the intended careful arrangement.

After about ten minutes a thin, pale young blonde in a Gucci suit emerged from the elevator bank and walked directly to me. She couldn't have missed me if she tried.

"Pleasure to meet you," she said. "I'm Emma, Mrs. Tremaine's assistant. She apologizes for not being here. She had to undergo surgery this week. Can you remind me about the purpose of your meeting?"

I had no idea what this Emma knew or didn't know about her boss, but I expected some kind of cover story like this.

"It's a personal matter," I said. "Perhaps you could get her on the phone and remind her that we met at the Villa Rosa Medical Facility last week, moments before her procedure. She promised to discuss her results with me before I proceed with my own. It's very important I speak with Margaret today. There have been reports of illicit behavior regarding our physician. The last thing either of us wants is to be caught up in bad press."

I had the feeling Emma, who I sensed was good at her job, wasn't buying any of it. Which was fine. I hadn't expected any assistant worth her salt to do so. All I needed was for her to realize I knew *something* of apparent importance to her boss; to take me seriously enough to get on the phone with Margaret Tremaine. Apparently she did.

"I'll see if I can reach her," Emma said. "Would you like some coffee? Water? Soda?"

"No, thank you. I'll just wait here. For as long as it takes."

The nefarious look I shot at Emma was meant to unnerve her, and would certainly be communicated with whatever else she told Mrs. Tremaine. Sure, she could summon security, but no one wants to have made the wrong call about a man in a wheel-chair. I was hopeful that I'd given her just enough rope to reel in Mrs. Tremaine.

Fifteen minutes later, Emma returned to the waiting area.

"Mrs. Tremaine is on her way in," she said with a forced smile. "Please come with me to her office."

She would not meet my eyes as I followed her past reception to an elevator, noting the surprised expression of my initial handler with the ponytail. It was just as well. It wouldn't have helped for Emma to see the look of relief that must be visible on my own face.

I wheeled down the busy top floor aisle behind her, past identically sized offices on my right all done in gray fabrics and brushed metal, dark wood, and muted black and white stone. Inside, well-dressed agents, their ties undone, barked passionately into telephones behind huge desks. Their assistants sat silently in cubicles on my left, listening in on the agents' conversations through earpieces and taking notes. The only color seemed to come from the art on the walls, including movie posters strategically placed to impress any newcomer.

"She's about ten minutes out," Emma told me when we reached Margaret Tremaine's office.

She ushered me inside. I set my brake and settled in to wait, watching Emma take a seat in her cubicle through narrow glass panels that framed Tremaine's office door. Then I looked around me.

In addition to the uniform black, white, and gray, Mrs. Tremaine's walls were lined with expensive, custom-built bookshelves that complemented the sleek design of the Florence Knoll desk and Mies van der Rohe chairs that all the CAA offices seemed to have. Books Tremaine had been responsible for turning into movies were prominently displayed; I knew many of the titles and authors' names. There were several audio books and a Dummies manual for a computer software voice recognition program. Margaret Tremaine specialized in acquiring books for film adaptations. She must wield quite a bit of power to have kept her job after losing her sight. I took a diet book designed for people with diabetes off the lowest shelf. It had never been opened, and now it would never have to be.

In the corner of my eye I saw Emma stand up. Mrs. Tremaine appeared, carrying her cane. Of course she wouldn't just waltz in. I was a monkey wrench in her plan—whatever it might be—to explain the successful "surgery" to her assistant. While Mrs. Tremaine exchanged pleasantries with Emma, Arthur glanced in through a glass panel and saw me. He whispered something in Tremaine's ear when she *tap-tapped* to her door, no doubt confirming that I was the one he'd mistaken for Desmond that first night. She came into the office alone, closing the door behind her and making her way carefully to her desk, where she sat down and collapsed her cane. She crossed her legs and leaned back in her chair. Beneath her oversized dark glasses I could see bandages covering her eyes.

"Well, Brandon, why have you dragged me all the way down here? Are you an actor?"

She spoke like the power broker she was. I was surprised by the edge in her voice, and hadn't expected the question.

"I used to be, but not anymore."

"Then what do you want from me, if it isn't a part in a film?"

"For starters, you can remove those glasses and bandages," I told her.

"I'm not about to do that. Why would you even ask me to?"

"Because I know you don't need them. I saw you when you went out on the fire escape in the moonlight after your last session with Desmond and Kyra. You didn't have your cane, and you had no problem avoiding that big space where the steps go down to the third floor. You were clearly drinking in everything in view, because you can see again."

She must have been surprised, but she was used to concealing any reactions she didn't want to reveal. She needed to be; it was part of doing business.

"Tell me what you want from me."

"I want answers."

"Answers to what? And why?"

"You asked if I'm an actor. I'll tell you why I'm not anymore.

It's because I'm in this fucking wheelchair. I was cast for a lead in a series right before a car crash broke my spine."

"Emma said your name sounded familiar," she interjected.

Fortunately, with the bandages still on, she couldn't see how perturbed I must look upon hearing this. I should have thought of that possibility.

"I have no life now, Mrs. Tremaine," I continued. "I want to walk again. And I believe that if Desmond and Kyra cured your blindness, they must be able to help me."

"You're talking about a miracle."

"I am, and if you don't answer my questions, I'll go to the press."

"Don't threaten me, Brandon. I'll call security and have you removed. It will be easy to convince everyone you're just an embittered actor."

"I'm sorry," I said. "But surely you can understand. Think of your own darkest moment of desperation. Then tell me you wouldn't make the same demands if our roles were reversed. I have no quarrel with you. All I want is a chance to be healed. It's all I can think about. I was about to throw myself off the roof when I saw you on that fire escape. I'm begging you. Help me and I'll never bother you again."

This was it, the moment of truth. I knew she could have me ejected and no one would believe anything I said, if only because I'd lied to get in to see her.

Her face softened. "You're right, I can see. I'll talk to you. But not for the reasons you think. I'll do it to protect them from your carelessness, and I'm not removing my bandages. My eyes are still sensitive to light. And it will look suspicious to Emma if we close my blinds. Ask me your questions, and I'll answer as fully as I can."

I wanted to believe her, but I knew that I didn't dare expose my ignorance. My first question had to be just right.

"How did you find them?"

"They found me. I was shopping with Arthur at the Bristol

Farms market. Kyra approached us. She put her hands over my eyes and said she could make me see again. I almost didn't go that night. But I wanted to believe her, and some voice deep inside me whispered that she was telling the truth. She said it would take three visits."

"Can you explain what Kyra and Desmond did to you in the apartment? How did the process work? Tell me everything. Spare no detail."

"They told Arthur and me to wait in the kitchen while they made love. They apologized, but said it was the only way. You know how small their place is. We couldn't avoid hearing them— we might as well have been in the room. I'll never get the sounds of her cries out of my head. They were like—"

"Birdsong," I finished for her.

"Exactly. When they were finished, Desmond brought me to the bed and laid me down beside Kyra. I could feel her hands on my face, so cool, and her soft breath, so warm and close to me. Then she was crying, straight into my eyes. Her tears came slowly, so hot they felt like they were burning me."

"She *cried* on you?"

"That's how it was done. After the first session I felt strange, but I still couldn't see. After the second, Arthur said he saw a difference in my eyes. After the third visit, I could see perfectly."

"And they promised you that you were completely healed? No chance of a relapse?"

"They didn't have to. I know it's permanent. I'm not a religious person, but I feel as though I've been touched by God."

Her voice was choked with emotion.

"And the price for the healing?"

"Five hundred thousand," she said. "In cash. Once my vision was restored, I was more than happy to pay it."

No wonder Desmond and Kyra were moving out with no concern for their deposit.

"Do you have any knowledge of how she does it? Or why she can?"

"I'll keep that to myself, if you don't mind."

"You realize all of this sounds crazy?" I said.

"Yes," she replied. "But it's true nonetheless."

"Thank you, Mrs. Tremaine." I said. "You won't be hearing from me again, I promise. And I'd appreciate it if we kept this between us, and you did not mention to Kyra or Desmond that we spoke."

"Agreed," she said. "And promise me you won't tell anyone else about them. If you do, they'll be hounded forever by anyone with an infirmity. She can't possibly heal the whole world."

"I promise."

"Good luck, Brandon. I hope you find the healing you're looking for. You're certainly tenacious enough."

CHAPTER 7

I left CAA more hopeful than any actor who'd just been signed as a client by the most powerful agency in the world. More than ever, I was desperate to be healed, desperate to walk again—and to prove that Mrs. Tremaine was right. That meant my future was in Kyra and Desmond's hands. Their continued absence from the Villa Rosa weighed heavily on me over the next two days. No doubt the pint of Gentleman Jack I consumed led to my next questionable act to retrieve evidence that what I wanted was not only possible but plausible.

I waited until I was sure that Kyra and Desmond were still not in their apartment and the lights were out in each of the other apartments on our floor—around 2:00 AM. Then I tried to jimmy their lock with a credit card—the old-fashioned way. No dice. I needed professional help. So I prepared a story—I'd lost my keys while out drinking at the Saddle Ranch or Cabo Cantina or the Trocadero—and called a locksmith. When he punched in my code on the keypad at the front gate, I answered my cell phone.

"Abe's Lock and Key. You called for a locksmith?"

"Fourth floor. Turn right when you leave the elevator."

Fortunately, neither the gate directory nor our mailboxes in the lobby—if he bothered to check—gave tenants' apartment numbers, only our names. I pressed 9 on my phone to buzz him in, and was sitting in front of Desmond and Kyra's apartment when he appeared in his gray work clothes, toolbox in hand.

"You Brandon?"

"Guilty," I said.

He considered my wheelchair. "You're lucky we're open 24/7. Do you have any picture ID on you?"

"I still have my driver's license from before my accident. But that was before I moved here," I said, praying that he wouldn't demand to see something with the Villa Rosa address.

"It'll do. I just need to confirm that you're the person in the digital directory at the security gate."

I produced the license from my wallet, concealing my relief.

"It'll be seventy-five dollars," he said. "You need to sign a waiver that I'm not responsible for any damage to the locks."

And that was that. I was both proud of and disgusted by how simple it was. My only concern was that Ray or Desmond or Kyra might suddenly appear as the locksmith went to work on the deadbolt. But they didn't, and within minutes he had the door open. I wheeled past him into the dark apartment and switched on the lights.

I was tremendously relieved to see Kyra and Desmond's belongings were still there.

"I'm moving some stuff into storage," I explained when I noticed the locksmith gazing inquisitively at the still-unopened cardboard cartons.

He grunted, and filled out paperwork. I handed him my credit card. He took the imprint, and after thanking me for my business and wishing me well, left. Now I just needed to not get caught.

Nervous and apprehensive, I locked the door. What to do next? I dared not stay a minute longer than absolutely necessary.

The apartment seemed several degrees warmer than my place. The air smelled of incense, mingled with Kyra's distinctive scent. All the laundry that had lain crumpled on the couch was now clean, pressed, and folded in neat stacks. The only things different were several candleholders spread throughout the room, including a half dozen or so on the coffee table, each bearing candles in various stages of melting. My first thought was of romantic evenings. Then I imagined healing spells or incantations. Was Kyra some sort of witch? Did the cartons contain exotic herbs, or substances not approved by the FDA that Kyra and Desmond had smuggled through customs? Kyra had told me they moved a lot, and now I wondered why. Were they healers on the run, trying to protect themselves from being hounded? That didn't seem like enough of a motive, but what did I know? Or was there some scientific explanation, something other than miraculous tears from sex magic to explain how Margaret Tremaine regained her sight? After all, she had been blind during the goings-on she'd described to me.

I remembered Mrs. Tremaine's half-million-dollar payment. Was the money stashed somewhere in this apartment? I could think of potential hiding spots, their place being the twin of my own. I wasn't interested in robbing them, although the amount of cash Desmond and Kyra required was a big issue for me. There was no way I could come up with it short of convincing my parents to mortgage their house. What would I say? "Hey, Dad, there's this girl who lives across the hall from me who can probably cure my paralysis with her tears. Can you mortgage the house to pay for it?" That wasn't likely to go over well. I'd deal with that when the time came.

I began my search.

The refrigerator was empty; the only food I found was a bowl of near-ripe figs on the counter. I opened the top drawer of a desk, hoping to find passports, an address book, a piece of forwarded mail, a business card or stray receipt, maybe half of an airline boarding pass—anything that might offer more information about who they were, where they'd come from, or where they might be headed next. There was nothing. The next drawer contained two promising items: a leather-bound journal and a small, flute-shaped instrument that was little more than a hollowed-out piece of wood with jagged, irregular holes in it.

I removed the journal with trembling fingers and flipped through page after page of beautifully handwritten notes, none of them in English. I assumed it was Kyra's and in her native language, whatever that might be. I wished I could take it with me to examine at length, then realized I could. I snapped pictures of several pages with my cell phone and carefully replaced the journal as I'd found it, next to the instrument I suspected to be the source of Kyra's unearthly music. It was hard to believe such gorgeous sounds could be produced through something so simple and crude. If only I could watch her play it.

Suddenly, I heard the door opening. How would I explain my presence? Even if they decided not to summon the police, surely my intrusion would be grounds to refuse their services and excommunicate me from their lives forever. But it was just my guilty imagination playing tricks on me.

Increasingly aware that I could get caught at any moment, I moved to the walk-in closet. A rolled-up towel jammed beneath the length of the door formed a makeshift seal. If I displaced it, it would be difficult to reposition exactly as I'd found it. I photographed it with my phone for reference, opened the door as carefully as possible to avoid shifting the towel too much, and maneuvered my wheelchair into the dark confines of the closet.

I strained to raise myself high enough to reach the light's pull chain. That didn't work. I pulled out my phone again and turned on the flashlight application, illuminating coats hanging on one side of a small, shelved space, and dresses, skirts, and sweaters on the other. A lot of the clothes, both male and female, were heavy winter garments. I rummaged through every pocket and found nothing useful, not even a telltale scrap of paper unconsciously deposited and forgotten. On the floor was a hodgepodge of shoes. One pair of Desmond's boots had well-worn spikes built into the soles. I had no idea what they were meant for. Tree climbing, perhaps? Maybe he was a lumberjack? I realized my right wheel was crushing one of Kyra's, a half boot. I dislodged it and molded the shoe back into shape as best I could.

I was hoping for a piece of luggage with an identity tag still attached. Instead I saw, at the rear of the closet, two black canvas duffel bags. Moving farther inside, I bent down, pulled the zipper on the first, and aimed the light at the contents. It was filled with mountain-climbing equipment: ropes, picks, carabiners, and the like. I had no problem picturing Desmond as a climber, and it explained the spiked shoes and his hooded parka. I zipped the bag closed and turned my attention to the other duffel.

The zipper on this one got caught on something after I opened it only an inch or two. I directed the light to it. Whatever was stuffed inside had been wrapped in plastic that now lodged in the zipper teeth. It smelled faintly rank. I feared that if I managed to completely unzip the bag and peel away the plastic, I'd never be able to hide the fact that it had been opened. But I'd come too far to stop now.

I wriggled the zipper gently until it finally came free of the plastic, then unzipped the bag one tiny tooth at a time. Holding the phone between my knees I aimed downward and proceeded to unwrap and disentangle layers of plastic.

My fingers brushed against something remarkably soft and silky. *Feathers!* Milk white with a grayish hue, matted yet remarkably moist. They seemed to fill the bag. The majority of the feathers were attached to a still-pliable skeletal framework; going by the shape, it must surely be the wing of some very large bird. Groping along, my fingers encountered a rough edge. I tugged it up from the bag for closer inspection. I could see scored bone, dried blood, and decayed sinew where the wing had been sheared off, by a saw I imagined, as the score marks were rough and uneven. I realized there were two wings in the bag, and estimated that they must each be at least five feet long; I couldn't risk removing them to find out. I examined the bone joints further, trying to imagine the sockets from which they'd been shorn. I noted the rounded, protruding, feathered edges. They seemed to have been rear-mounted, likely attached to the scapula, like those of a bat. What type of bird had such rear-mounted wings? I was curious to see the rest of the creature.

A disturbing memory from the party before the accident suddenly came back to me, of a little curly-haired girl in a glittery costume with big puffy wings, glaring up at me ...

Not a bird.

An angel!

Out of nowhere an impossible image sprang into my mind: a figure standing erect, wings opening wide behind it.

What was I thinking? I tried to dismiss the insane notion as the Jack Daniels whispering in my brain. But it refused to be dispelled. What else could I be holding in my hands? Who had done this? Was this some kind of terrible trophy? What sort of malevolence was I dealing with?

Suddenly I was terrified, desperate to escape, shaking so badly it was difficult to aim the phone light and take pictures of the ghastly severed appendages. Somehow I managed, then refolded the plastic and zipped up the duffel bag, all the while fighting to overcome the impulse to flee to the security of my own apartment.

Badly as I wanted simply to rush away, I first had to cover my tracks. I forced myself to back out of the closet, doing my best to replace the shoes as I'd found them, cursing myself for not having photographed the haphazard positions in which they'd lain. I closed the closet door an inch at a time, carefully guiding the rolled-up towel with my hands to keep it in place. I reviewed the photo I had taken and adjusted the towel to match it.

My courage waning, I made myself take a final look around. Once I left, there would be no coming back. My heart pounded. My armpits were soaked with sweat. I told myself everything would be all right. I'd put things back as I'd found them. No one had seen me. All that was left to do now was switch off the lights, lock the door, and cross the hall.

I turned the doorknob, terrified that the door wouldn't open. Or, worse, that if it did someone would be standing there waiting, ready to accost me. The hallway was empty. Relieved, I twisted the turn button on the knob to set the lock, rolled out to the hall and closed the door behind me.

That was when I realized the fatal flaw in my plan; I couldn't reset the deadbolt from the outside. There was nothing I could do about it now. As if this wasn't bad enough, my own apartment door was ajar. Had I left it that way? I simply couldn't remember.

I entered my studio in a panic, hurriedly turning on all the lights and checking everywhere to make sure no one had entered during my absence. I tried to assure myself I was safe, but I couldn't. I might never feel safe again. I had touched something inhuman in Desmond and Kyra's possession, and now, somehow, they seemed less than human as well. Where the hell had the wings come from, and from what? Were Desmond and Kyra monsters or hunters of monsters? One thing was certain; there was true darkness in the world. And now that I'd become aware of it, was I damned?

My throat tightened. My stomach heaved. Rushing into the bathroom, I gripped the cold porcelain toilet basin and regurgitated. Afterward my nose and throat burned; my eyes watered so badly I could barely see.

Exhausted, I wheeled myself back into the kitchen. I had no idea what to do next. I didn't want to be cured anymore. Let me remain paralyzed; I just needed to be safe from Desmond and Kyra.

The sound of someone trying to unlatch one of my front windows startled me. I sat frozen. Something knocked against the window on the opposite side of the room. Screwing up my courage, I rolled over and quickly drew back the curtains. Nothing. Just the distant lights of downtown Los Angeles, the towering palms swaying violently in the hot Santa Ana winds. I was certain there were demons out there trying to get in, but were they only in my mind? I was just rational enough to grasp that the situation was irrational.

But I couldn't sleep in the apartment. I needed to find someplace safe to spend the night.

CHAPTER 8

*J*gathered my laptop and phone charger into my backpack, grabbed a denim coat, and was out of the Villa Rosa gate as quickly as my wheelchair would take me. Looking back, I noted that all the apartments were dark. For the briefest moment, I thought I saw a shadowy figure on the roof staring down at me. I watched for further movement but detected none.

I headed west on Sunset, wary of every passing car, unable to shake the feeling that someone—or some*thing*—was following me. The Santa Ana buffeted me in my wheelchair, rocked streetlights on their wires, and shook the giant palms along the boulevard. There were very few cars at that hour and no foot traffic, which I attributed to the wind. I turned left at La Cienega, my destination the always-open International House of Pancakes on Santa Monica, a decent distance from the Villa Rosa.

The struggle against the wind to keep control of the wheelchair going three blocks downhill dispelled any traces of inebriation that might still have remained. I was feeling somewhat calmer by the time I finally arrived at IHOP.

"Just one?" asked the pockmarked hostess, and offered me my choice of booths.

I looked around. The restaurant was sparsely populated. An elderly couple sipping soup and not speaking to each other. A young couple holding hands. A foursome of late-night party kids spilling things and generally making asses of themselves. And a couple of single patrons drinking coffee and typing on laptops, no doubt writing scripts that would never even be seen by someone capable of making them into films. All of them separated by lots of space. I pointed to the farthest booth in the back, against the wall with no windows.

The hostess led me to it and handed me a menu after I maneuvered myself out of my chair. Seeing me remove my laptop from my backpack, she provided me with IHOP's Wi-Fi password, then sent over my waitress, a tired blonde no older than myself. I wasn't hungry, but I intended to stay until daylight. Then I would call Father Tom, the only person I could talk to about what I'd seen. I wondered what the other patrons would think if I told them. Of course, I didn't. Instead I ordered breakfast, to pay for my seat, and requested a full pot of coffee. Minutes later the waitress placed my food on the table beside the computer and retreated into the kitchen.

I began my search for proof I wasn't losing my mind with broad categories. "Angels" and "demons" invariably led to pages dealing with exorcisms and the requirements for sainthood. To my surprise, the Roman Catholic Church was the most pragmatic about these subjects. Reports of alleged encounters with angels gave me little confidence in their authenticity. "Demonic encounters" left me with none; as often as not, they referenced novels by Stephen King or H. P. Lovecraft.

I became engrossed in diagrams and images reputedly of the anatomy of angels and how the wings are attached at the shoulder blades. More than a few depicted how they might appear when severed. I pulled my phone from my pocket, fearing that the pictures I had taken would still be there and equally fearful they would not. I needed to see them, and longed for confirmation that they were not unique, that someone else had firsthand evidence of the existence of what I'd seen. But I found no photos, avian or otherwise, remotely resembling the grainy pictures in my phone (overexposed due to the flash in the pitch-dark closet). Seeing them again only amplified my terror, even as I worried that I was somehow alerting a dark menace of my exact location.

Forcing myself to stop looking at the ghastly wings, I noticed that I'd finished my pot of coffee. I signaled the waitress to bring another, and moved on to "exorcism."

The Church lists speaking or writing in ancient tongues as one of the requisite signs an exorcism is needed. I scrolled backward to the photos of Kyra's journal. Surely it qualified, but for what? Of what exactly did I think she might be guilty? Playing heavenly music? Healing people? According to the Church, to proclaim anyone a saint required two verified healings. But that was after the would-be saint had died. Kyra was alive. How many people besides Mrs. Tremaine had she healed? If the wings were evidence of some slaughter, who or what had been slaughtered—and why? As far as I could see, the Church made no provision for someone like Kyra, nor could I find reference of any sort to the healing power of tears.

The answers might lie in her journal. I wished I could scan the photos of her handwritten pages or retype the symbols into a translation program and find out what they meant. The best I could determine was that it was some form of bastardized Hebrew, a language with which I was entirely unfamiliar.

This led me to the mystical history of Hebrew. In the Garden of Eden, Adam spoke to angels in a secret language that was lost when he and Eve were cast out after eating the fruit of the Tree of Knowledge. Eventually Adam came to speak in an amalgamated language of heavenly and earthly words to his own family. This evolved into biblical Hebrew, the only language spoken until the destruction of the Tower of Babel, when God confounded humans with multiple languages to stop us from working together and climbing to Heaven. Was Kyra's writing ancient Hebrew, or some lost variant thereof? For all I knew, I could be in possession of another Rosetta Stone.

In this way hours passed. Suddenly I became aware of a din of voices around me. I looked up from my computer.

The restaurant was crowded with morning diners. Sunlight poured in through the windows. My dishes had been cleared from the table; all that remained was an empty coffee mug with the check underneath it. I did not recognize any of the wait staff; I presumed the shift had changed. I had survived the night.

It was time to surrender my tiny will to a higher power. If the severed wings in the closet were real—and I believed they were —then I had to concede there were agents of darkness in the world. And if there were agents of darkness in the world, I had to have faith there were agents of light here as well.

I sent Father Tom a text message: PLEASE CONTACT ME IMMEDIATELY. URGENT WE MEET. BRANDON.

Seconds later his response flashed reassuringly: ABOUT TO CONDUCT MORNING SERVICE. WILL CONTACT YOU IMMEDI- ATELY AFTERWARD. TOM.

I told myself everything would be all right now. Father Tom would come, and I'd confess everything to him: my first observa- tions of Desmond, my meetings with Kyra, Mrs. Tremaine's blindness, the locksmith—all my deceptions leading to my grue- some discovery in Desmond and Kyra's apartment. Then I would show him the photos and tell him everything I suspected from my IHOP research. Father Tom would know exactly what to do next. I was counting on it.

Relieved, I signaled to a pretty young waitress with my coffee mug. She scurried over.

"Rough night?" she asked as she refilled the mug with steaming liquid.

"Yeah," I responded. "I'm hoping for a better day."

The cries of a wailing baby in the next booth jarred me awake. I lifted my head from atop my hands on the table, realizing I'd fallen asleep. The mother glanced at me apologetically as she hushed her infant.

My coffee was cold in the mug. I looked down at my phone beside it. Father Tom had called several times, and finally, about twenty minutes ago, left a text message: I'M AT THE VILLA ROSA. WHERE ARE YOU?

Of course he had gone there when I didn't respond. Groggily, I texted him back: ON MY WAY. PLEASE WAIT FOR ME DOWNSTAIRS.

I paid my check, put my laptop in my backpack, maneuvered myself into my cripple wagon, and made my way east on Santa Monica Boulevard, my arms thrusting the wheels forward harder than ever before in the blazing sun. At Fairfax I paused to catch my breath, then began the climb to Sunset. By the time I reached the Villa Rosa, I was out of breath again and sweating profusely.

Father Tom was nowhere in sight. Someone must have opened the gate for him. I looked up. Desmond and Kyra's corner window was open. This could be bad, very bad.

My heart pounded in my chest as I exited the elevator and saw that the hallway was empty. As if on cue, Desmond, handsome as ever in black chinos, a black T-shirt, and a low-hanging green fatigue army jacket, stepped from his doorway.

"There he is," he called out. "We've been looking for you, Brandon. Come on in here."

His use of the word "we" chilled me. Then I heard Father Tom and Kyra laughing inside the apartment.

My hands gripped my wheels tightly. I mustered a pleasant smile and rolled silently forward; it seemed to take forever to steer my way down the hall. Desmond scrutinized me with a forced grin, his dark eyes piercing me as I approached. When I got close, he put a finger to his lips and drew back the edge of his jacket, revealing a Colt .45 tucked in his waistband. I'd carried one just like it, loaded with blanks of course, in a short film I'd done. I doubted very much that Desmond's gun held blanks. I gritted my teeth and suppressed the urge to spin the chair around and book it out of there fast as I could.

He held the door open as I wheeled inside. I wondered if I would be wheeling back out under my own power or atop a gurney under a bloodstained sheet.

Father Tom was sitting at the kitchen table in his usual black shirt, white priest's collar, and jeans, a mug of coffee before him. He gave me a warm smile as I entered the apartment. Kyra stood on the opposite side of the counter, stunning as always, in a long cotton summer dress. She smiled as well, though her eyes betrayed accusation and warning.

Desmond closed the door behind me and ambled across the room to stand beside Kyra, resting his arms calmly on the counter. The hair went up on the back of my neck. He reminded me of a disgruntled sharpshooter from some western.

"Sorry I wasn't here when you arrived, Father," I said.

"No problem, Brandon," he replied. "Desmond heard me knocking on your door and invited me to wait here. I welcomed the opportunity to meet your lovely friends. Kyra was just telling me how they met at the Wailing Wall in Jerusalem."

That made sense. A good cover story would be that she was simply Israeli. In case I'd already revealed my suspicions to Father Tom, and her journal turned out to be written in prehistoric Hebrew.

"Now, Desmond," Father Tom continued. "Would I be wrong to assume it was love at first sight?"

"No," he said. "I fell madly in love the first moment I saw her."

"Are you Jewish as well?"

"I was raised Catholic, but I'm an agnostic now. I believe that there's a God, but I don't think any religion has gotten the story quite right."

"And you, Kyra? Are you a believer as well?"

"Yes, Father," she answered with the utmost confidence, then turned her attention to me. "What I don't believe in is men who proclaim His will to try and justify their crimes against a neighbor."

Father Tom followed her gaze. I could only imagine how I looked, uncombed and unshaven in yesterday's clothes, reeking of sweat.

"You look like you haven't slept, Brandon," he said with true concern. "Your text sounded urgent. Is something going on?"

I quickly considered my options. The braver part of me wanted to confront Desmond and Kyra with this man of God present. Let them try to explain away the contents of their closet and Mrs. Tremaine's testimony. I knew I would sound insane to Father Tom, and I dared not produce my pictures without risking Desmond drawing his gun. If Kyra were mine, I would do anything to protect her.

Before I could decide how to proceed, Desmond responded for me.

"He's afraid to admit it's his drinking, Father," he said gently, his delivery so perfect I could have applauded him. "He's gotten out of control the past few days. He even confessed to us he'd considered suicide."

The thought flashed through my mind that somehow he knew about my going to the roof the night of Mrs. Tremaine's last session. Had she told him about my confronting her after promising not to? It was uncanny. Desmond had just set up an explanation for my possible demise in the guise of an Alcoholics Anonymous intervention.

Bless Father Tom. His look neither accused nor condemned me.

"I'm sorry to hear that, Brandon. You're lucky to have such good friends. I'm glad you called me—that required courage. I'll take you to a meeting today and we'll find you a sponsor."

"Let us take him," Desmond offered, again before I could speak. "We'd be more than happy to, if Brandon agrees." He shot me a look at once sympathetic and baleful. "There's a meeting just down the street on Fairfax we pass all the time."

I hesitated, and they could all see it. Father Tom must have taken it for reluctance to enter the program. He couldn't know I was terrified of what would happen if he left me in their care.

Kyra came and knelt before my wheelchair, grasping my sweaty palms in her cool hands and looking into me with her soulful gray eyes.

"Let us help you, Brandon," she pleaded.

"All right," I said, unable to deny her even though I might be signing my own death warrant.

CHAPTER 9

ather Tom finished his coffee and said his goodbyes. I was thankful for his safety as the door closed behind him, even as I feared for my own. Desmond stepped over to me, his hand resting casually on the handle of the gun.

"That was a wise choice, Brandon," he said. "Now we have to talk."

I had not been granted the opportunity to make a final confession to my priest, so I offered it now to Desmond and Kyra, blabbering through my crimes against them and what I surmised and suspected, omitting only my longing for Kyra. But I knew that she silently filled in those details.

"Who else have you told about this?" Desmond demanded.

I considered lying and offering names, wondering if that might be my best course for survival. If he believed others knew, it might stay his hand. But I felt compelled to be truthful.

"No one," I answered. "I swear it on my life."

Desmond scrutinized me coldly.

"He's telling the truth," Kyra said. "I can hear it in his voice."

Desmond accepted her word without question. She motioned to him. They went into the kitchen and began whispering heatedly, intermittently glancing at me. I wondered if I could escape. Could I overpower Desmond and wrest the gun from him? Failing that, could I at least get out the door, so that in the event he shot me it might be witnessed, or more difficult to conceal? Perhaps I should begin shouting loudly for help, and hope some other tenant might hear me and call the police.

Before I could decide on a course of action, Desmond crossed back to me, aiming the gun at my face.

"You've left us no choice," he said. "We've decided to heal you. But if you don't do exactly as I order, you'll wish that I had shot you."

"I'll do whatever you tell me to," I choked out, straining to believe what I'd just heard. "Can I ask—"

Desmond cut me off.

"No, you can't. We'll tell you what you need to know and what to do. You can start by getting us something to eat. We have no food and we're on a ridiculously tight schedule that you've just made even tighter."

He was letting me leave, confident that I would return—and he was right. After all my deceptions, he was offering me salvation. He knew I would do anything he asked to be able to walk again, no matter if it were through medical science or methods arcane. I wondered why he didn't simply order in, but I wasn't about to challenge Desmond now. Maybe he and Kyra needed me out of the way for a while.

Kyra was beaming. Somehow, I knew the decision to heal me was hers, and had been all along. She was the special one. Desmond was her guardian, her provider, her lover. He would do whatever she requested of him.

"Any preferences?" I asked.

"I like figs," Kyra said.

"Just make sure there's plenty of protein," Desmond added. "And nothing with wings."

Somehow that made perfect sense.

I headed next door to Bristol Farms with tears in my eyes, thankful to be alive.

We sat at their kitchen table sharing assorted deli meat, French bread, Gruyere cheese, and dried figs I'd selected. Kyra only seemed interested in the figs, which she ate one by one.

"Here's the deal, Brandon," Desmond began. "You want to be healed and we can heal you. But it's going to take time we don't have, and if we make time, you're putting us at risk. Serious risk."

I thought about the dreadful contents of the closet, and wondered how they might fit into the risk, but knew better than to ask.

"I don't have the kind of money that Mrs. Tremaine paid you," I said.

"We require something else," Desmond said. "And it's not going to be easy for you. I need to become you. That means borrowing your identity—driver's license, passport, Social Security number, credit cards, cell phone. Everything. And you're going to have to work hard to remain invisible while I do it."

"I'll have a difficult time without my credit card," I said.

"I'm leaving you a hundred thousand dollars. Set your rent and all your regular bills on autopay from your account. Buy some American Express travelers checks and use cash for every-thing else. I'll make periodic deposits to cover any charges we make, and let you know when you can report the credit card missing. You'll just need to lie low, be cautious, and stay low-tech."

"For how long?"

"About six months. It's not as hard as you might think. I'll give you a crash course on how to live under the radar. It will seem like you've gone on vacation."

It could work. I'd already isolated myself from my old life. I'd find a way to handle it. Six months wasn't such a long time.

"I'll do it," I said.

"I'm not finished, Brandon. There's one other thing you need to agree to. Without it there's no deal."

I steeled myself.

"Kyra also needs a new identity. You have to get your friend Bethany to loan us her driver's license, passport, and Social Security number. We don't need her credit card, but she has to stop using it until you hear from us. And she can't know what you know. So you'll have to remain in your wheelchair, even though you won't need it. If she agrees, she gets two hundred thousand dollars with no strings attached. All she has to do is remain quiet and invisible."

"She's in school," I told them. "That might be a problem."

"She should be willing to take the time off for two hundred thousand."

"I'll convince her," I said.

"I'm counting on it," Desmond said. "But you've got to move fast. You'll undergo your first treatment this evening. Bring Bethany's and your documents with you. Be here at midnight."

"And in three treatments I'll be able to walk again? And to ..."

Kyra, who had not said a word during the entire conversation, responded.

"Yes," she said. "You'll be able to do both."

"Screw us up in the slightest and you'll be thinking about your time in that chair as the good old days," Desmond added. "Understand, Brandon?"

"I understand," I said.

"Good," said Desmond. "This is your lucky day."

After Desmond finished giving me his "crash course," I felt confident that I could pull it off. Now I just had to get Bethany on board. I went straight to her apartment, and presented her with Desmond's offer, inwardly praying that she'd go for it.

"I don't know, Brandon," Bethany said when I finished. "I've been down this road before. I loaned my credit card to a friend who asked me to wait a week before reporting it stolen. Some expensive items were purchased. The credit card company expunged me of responsibility but only after a tremendous amount of hassle. They canceled the card and wouldn't issue me a new one. I realize Desmond and Kyra aren't asking for a credit card, but the rest? Did they tell you why they want it?"

"They just need to disappear. They can't say why, but I believe them."

"Are you sure they're not cops or something?"

"I'd stake my life on it."

"I'd have to quit school for a semester."

"You can take a leave of absence."

"I suppose."

"With two hundred thousand dollars you can pay off your entire student loan. You wouldn't have to see clients unless you wanted to."

"That sounds nice. And they're paying me in cash? That's over a thousand dollars a day for doing nothing."

"If you think about it, they're the ones who'd have to worry. We could report our ID being stolen at any time, and they'd be screwed. They couldn't prove we were lying."

Of course, Bethany had no way of knowing I would never do such a thing. But I needed to convince her. I didn't know what I would do if she refused.

"Do you trust them, Brandon?"

"I do. Really, Bethany."

She looked at me intently for a few minutes, her forehead scrunched as she thought the matter through. My muscles tensed. I was desperate to plead with her yet terrified of saying the wrong thing. So I kept quiet, figuring I could make another attempt to convince her to help if she turned me down now.

Her brow cleared.

"I trust you, Brandon," she said. "If you're gonna do it, I will too."

I wilted with relief in my chair.

"I've thought long and hard," I assured her. "I want to do it."

"Then it's settled."

I had to stop myself from hugging her with joy, for fear she'd recognize my desperation and relief for what they were.

I knocked on Desmond and Kyra's door at exactly midnight. Desmond opened as far as the chain permitted. I passed him an envelope containing Bethany's and my driver's licenses and passports, my credit card, and a slip of paper containing both our Social Security numbers. He told me to wait a moment, and closed the door. I heard their muffled voices speaking inside. Then the door reopened, the chain still in place.

"All right. Come back in fifteen minutes," Desmond said, and shut the door again.

After fifteen of the most unnerving minutes of my life, Desmond gestured me inside. He was now wearing a long white terrycloth robe such as you might find at a spa or an upscale hotel. The apartment lights were off, in contrast to the bright lights of the hall. My eyes took a moment to adjust to the dozens of burning candles, the majority of them near the open bed. Kyra emerged from the bathroom barefoot in an identical robe, her hair pulled back in a ponytail. She bent down to me, said my name, and kissed my cheek. Taking control of my wheelchair from behind, Desmond steered me into the kitchen, out of view of the bed.

"You know what we're going to do," he said.

"Couldn't I wait at my place until you're ready for me?" I asked, ashamed and embarrassed. The thought that they would be having sex a few feet away from me was unendurable.

"Unfortunately, no. There's no other way to provoke her tears, and they only flow for a few brief moments. Believe me, if there were some other way, we wouldn't do it like this. Take off your shirt. When we're done, I'll bring you to the bed. She needs to make contact with the injury on your spine."

"I can show her where the break is," I said.

"That won't be necessary," he said. "She'll know."

He placed his hand on my shoulder in a gesture I realized, with a shock, was meant to comfort. This, after I'd effectively betrayed them, uncovered their secrets, forced them to agree to heal me, and, it seemed, put them at what Desmond described as "very serious" risk. He hadn't specified what the risk was, but I was certain he wasn't exaggerating. His compassion humbled me.

"This won't take nearly as long as I'd like," he said before I could thank him. "We just don't have the time. Make sure you're ready when I come back for you."

He left me in the dark kitchen. The darkness kept me from seeing what they were doing, but not from hearing it. Only the counter separated the kitchen from the living area and the opened Murphy bed. I was intensely aware of everything—the sound of Desmond's footsteps crossing the floor, the faint *whoosh* of the mattress compressing as he knelt down on it, the rustle of sheets as Kyra shifted, pushing them aside, and, finally, the unmistakable whisper of flesh against flesh as she pulled him into her arms.

They exchanged soft words I couldn't discern as I followed Desmond's directions, wriggling out of my unbuttoned shirt. More rustlings and whispers as the two became more intimately entwined. I heard Kyra sigh, and knew Desmond was inside her. Jealousy and regret, longing and shame, cut into me. Soon the sounds of his quick, heavy breathing mingled with her escalating moans. I remembered my dream in which they both held my hands. This was more intense. I thought I heard the way the sheets moved beneath them, heard the way his hips were thrusting, driving him into her, heard the slide of her hands down his arms, around his back, heard her lift her legs to wrap them around him, and pull him closer—imagining not what it felt like to be Desmond, but what Kyra must be feeling as he took her, as if she had somehow opened her mind to me as she opened her body to Desmond. It was as if I was in the bed with them, part of their lovemaking, uneasily twined between them. It wasn't their skin against mine, yet somehow it was more intimate. Desmond was inside her and she was somehow inside me, inside my head. I never felt so naked, so raw and exposed.

Their pace quickened. Tension mounted. Kyra shrieked like a wounded bird, so loud and piercingly I shuddered. Gooseflesh covered my arms. I clutched my chair rails hard; I could scarcely feel my fingers. Kyra cried out again. I pictured some ancient, long-winged bird locked in congress with her mate high in the sky, wings beating and fluttering as they plummeted at crushing velocity to the ground. At the last possible moment before they hit, a final terrified cry issued from her throat. Their mating finished, he released his gripping talons.

I was shaking. Sweat dripped from every pore of my body.

Suddenly Desmond was behind me, guiding me to the bed. I clasped my hands around his neck as he quickly lifted me from the chair to lie beside Kyra. She was only partially covered by her robe, still breathing heavily, tears wet on her cheeks.

"On his stomach, head toward me on the pillow," she whispered.

The sheets were rife with her scent. Kyra bent close and laid her soft, cool cheek against my spine at the small of my back. Her hair weighed against me. She moved her head lower, to the spot dividing the parts of me that could feel from those that couldn't. Her body trembled. She emitted a sob. I assumed her tears were falling but could not feel them. I imagined her silently telling me everything would be all right.

As Desmond had warned me, her tears fell for only a few moments. I knew they had ceased when Kyra sat up, adjusted her robe, and made her way quickly to the bathroom.

"Just lie there quietly a while," Desmond said as I heard the door close.

He was standing out of view in the kitchen, opening and

shutting drawers. The shower started running. Desmond ignited a burner on the stove. Sometime later a spoon clinked against porcelain.

"It should be okay to get up now," he said.

I maneuvered myself into the wheelchair, found my shirt and buttoned it back on, then joined him in the kitchen. He offered me a mug of aromatic steaming liquid.

"It's mulled wine," he said. "A mix of red wine, raisins, and spices. We drink it back home to kill the cold. I know it's hot as hell here, but I find it soothing."

The drink was delicious. My body welcomed the infusion of warm alcohol. I decided not to ask where back home was.

"How do you feel?" he asked.

"Relaxed," I said. "But not any different physically." Actually, I felt close to Kyra and Desmond. Despite the strangeness of the situation and regardless of the outcome, the intimacy of the attempt was profoundly comforting. "Does it always work?"

"She's only ever failed to heal one person, an old man who was days from death's door. She said it was his time. That he was already in God's hands."

"Do you believe that? That God has reasons for allowing some people to be sick and others to be healed?"

I really wanted to hear his thoughts on the matter. Instead he changed the subject.

"I'm sure you'll see marked improvement after the second treatment."

I decided to ask him about something else I really wanted to know.

"Why do you need to keep moving? Is it to avoid being overwhelmed by people who want help? Like me?"

Desmond paused, and concentrated on sipping from his mug. Finally he spoke.

"It's not personal. People are easy enough to deal with. But we still need to be extremely careful about who we let into our lives."

We were interrupted by the sound of Kyra turning off the shower. Desmond retrieved the mug from my hands and took it to the sink.

"You'd better get some sleep," he said. "Be here same time tomorrow night. And don't shave. I'd like you to grow out your beard. I'll be shaving mine off."

CHAPTER 10

J wheeled myself to the door, one eye on the closet, alarm bells sounding in my head. Had I imagined there was something odd in the way Desmond said "people"? A subtle emphasis suggesting that he and Kyra might be hiding from something *besides* human beings? I thought of the contents of the second duffel bag. I was in unimaginable territory, exhausted from not having slept the night before and all the stress that followed. I'd gone from being certain I would die to what felt like the sure promise of healing. Too much that was inexplicable had happened, and I'd gone with too little sleep to think about any of this stuff rationally. I stripped out of my clothes quickly and hauled myself into bed, almost instantly falling asleep.

I walked through tall grass in an unfamiliar meadow, toward a grove of trees. Ahead of me, obscured from view, I heard a man and woman arguing. I cleared the grass and saw Kyra and Desmond lying naked in a patch of leaves. I stepped back, using the grass as cover, and watched them.

Desmond's hands gripped Kyra's upper arms, their gazes locked. Her words poured forth in a quick, passionate torrent; I couldn't distinguish exactly what she was saying. It was clear she was trying to convince Desmond of something. He looked uncertain and worried, as if whatever she was saying frightened him. Suddenly he closed his eyes and groaned like a man in unbearable pain. When he opened them again a moment later, it was as if some invisible barrier had fallen. His jaw set in steely determination. He pulled her into his arms and kissed her exactly like the first kiss I had seen them exchange—a meeting of souls as well as mouths. Desmond and Kyra lost themselves completely in it. I could have walked right up to them and they wouldn't have noticed me.

Suddenly my perspective shifted. I now was Desmond, Kyra wrapped in my arms, every cell in my body aching for her.

One kiss had by now become a series of kisses. Her long fingers, quick and nimble, traced over the planes of my face, the slope of my shoulders, the length of my back as my hands gently explored her body. And that was exactly what it was: exploration, discovery, learning the body of a new lover. The watcher in me realized this was Desmond and Kyra's first time together. I was filled with wonder at the softness of her skin, the lithe perfection of her body, the unique perfume of her scent, the honeyed taste of her mouth as Kyra lifted her legs to wrap around my waist, shifting and rising to sit astride me and impale herself on the hot, hard length of me. The kisses stopped then. She threw her head back with a soft cry of ecstasy. I leaned forward groaning, burying my face in the crook of her neck as we began the ancient dance, our movements slow and deep and long as we savored every writhing thrust, every devouring touch, knitting our souls as one together in a never-to-be-broken bond. We held hands as Kyra rocked her thin hips, approaching climax. She began her birdlike cries of pleasure.

And something unseen cried back—a rage-filled, discordant cawing nothing like Kyra's pleasured birdsong.

Kyra rolled off me, gazing skyward with dread. Terrified, I tried to follow the jarring sound's trajectory, to see what the animal was. But the sun obscured my vision, first dazzling me, then driving me into darkness.

I woke up shaking, back in my apartment. To calm myself, I looked at the dream logically. I was infatuated with Kyra, assumed she and Desmond were being pursued, had observed their arcane healing methods, and had found a pair of severed wings in their closet. I wanted to understand what was going on, and my unconscious had simply blended these elements together. Desmond had spoken of risk, but he hadn't said danger. I told myself that the only people likely to be chasing my neighbors were others longing for healing, and maybe the Internal Revenue Service, that the risk was either of being overwhelmed with requests for help or being handed stiff penalties for failing to report most of their taxable income. Even so, the feeling that Kyra and Desmond were in actual physical danger lingered.

The morning sun filtered in from the east through the curtains of my corner window. I was thrilled to hear Kyra playing her beautiful music across the hall. I spent the day resting, telling myself not to overthink the situation, to just be grateful. Why look for trouble? The fact was, as long as whatever they did made me whole again, I didn't care if they stole my identity, kept the money, charged a million dollars to my credit card, and royally screwed me over. And if they screwed Bethany over as well, I'd find a way to make it up to her. As midnight approached it was impossible to quell my feeling of anticipation.

Desmond received me warmly into the candlelit apartment. Kyra was in bed, also robed. The majority of the cardboard boxes were gone; the couple was leaving the Villa Rosa after my third session.

"Looks like you're almost moved out," I said.

"Almost," Kyra said, smiling at me. "And thanks to you we've booked passage to our next destination." She turned to Desmond and said, "I'm ready."

Desmond sat beside her and took her hands in his. I wheeled myself into the kitchen and poured myself a glass of water, letting the tap run for a few minutes, trying to mask the sounds of their lovemaking. It didn't work. Everything—the footsteps, the mattress and sheets, the whispered voices, the slide of flesh against flesh—was all as clear as it had been the night before. Once again, I felt as if Kyra had opened her mind to me, was sharing her experience, drawing me mentally if not physically into their lovemaking. Again, I felt humbled. How remarkable it was that Desmond could share Kyra as he did. I wondered if their pleasure was somehow diminished or enhanced by a stranger being present. I would never know, and frankly it didn't matter. Their rhythm and timing were much as they had been the first time, though I felt a little less embarrassed.

Kyra began crying out. Suddenly I was in last night's dream. The giant shadow swooped down, its massive wings beating.

"Get over here now, Brandon," Desmond yelled, snapping me back to the present.

I ripped off my shirt as I sped from the kitchen to the bed. Desmond pulled me atop the covers, helping me twist into position on my stomach beside Kyra. She laid her head on my back and shuddered.

And then I *felt* them: drops of liquid fire on my back. I would have pulled away, but she grasped my waist and locked me in place. She seemed impossibly strong. The tears kept falling. I writhed to escape the burning, but couldn't dislodge myself. And it wasn't simply my skin that burned. Each searing drop seemed to burrow into my pores, down to my bones. The moment I could no longer stand the pain, she stopped crying. The burning began to subside.

We lay there catching our breath. I was wonderstruck. In places insensate since the accident, I could now feel Kyra's hair like a spreading web, her eyelashes fluttering against my skin, her cool cheek, her hands clasping my waist. But these victories were insignificant compared to the one between my legs. I felt myself stiffen and grow furiously hard against the covers. I had to force myself to just lie there, to not slide my hand down for proof. I felt a pang of guilt toward Desmond, who had fallen asleep on the other side of the bed. I savored the sensation of Kyra's head resting on the small of my back.

I sensed that she knew all of this. After a moment she lifted her head off me. I opened my eyes. The front of her robe had nearly completely parted; her perfect, pear-shaped breasts glistened with sweat, the nipples erect. She sleepily saw me looking; her eyes acknowledged my stare without a trace of modesty as she turned to spoon herself against Desmond's sleeping body.

As she was shifting the white terrycloth to cover her back, I saw two deep gashes, one on each shoulder blade—pink, puffed scar tissue rough along the edges like they had been cauterized.

A strange calmness settled over me. The wounds marked the joints where her wings once connected—the wings in the bag in her closet. I surrendered to the idea that Kyra was an angel.

I was walking through the same tall grass, toward the same grove of trees. I quickened my pace when I heard Kyra and Desmond in their passionate exchange. As I arrived at the clearing, I witnessed them just as I had before, staring intently at each other while Kyra made her impassioned plea—but not Kyra as I knew her. This was Kyra as she must have been before she lost her wings. They spread behind her, magnificent and full. And somehow she was not a heavenly angel but an altogether sensual earthly creature.

This time I knew it to be a dream, and made no attempt to hide my presence. I willed myself to become Desmond. My perspective changed, but not as I'd wished it. I was looking at Desmond, who stared back at me with that determined look. There was a delicious, foreign feeling in the muscles of my back and shoulders—as my wings fluttered—stirring the long grass around us. I was Kyra, and though as Brandon I had never spent a moment wondering about my gender identity, now I was wholly, perfectly female. Perfectly Kyra. And Kyra wanted, with an indescribable ache of desire, and in defiance of everything she'd been raised to believe or expect about her place and purpose in the world, to become one with Desmond. Before, I had felt Kyra's lips yielding to the demands made by mine. Now I felt the pleasure of yielding. Where my hands had reveled in the softness of her skin and plump fullness of her breasts, I now shivered under these caresses, my nipples tightening in desire. And where I had pressed my length into the welcoming depths of her wet core, it was my core now that was swiftly entered and deliciously filled—and my wings beating with unspeakable joy. I rocked my hips wantonly, overcome with lust and starving for completion. The birdlike cries began, and I was making them. I grew frightened, fearing that if I continued my cries would surely be answered.

But it was already too late. Something shrieked back.

I rolled off Desmond, searching the sky for the source of that terrifying sound. Again the large, winged shadow passed overhead and across the meadow. I tried to see what it was, but the sun obscured my vision. A word formed on my lips—Kyra's lips.

"Azareal."

Kyra shook my shoulder violently. I woke to find myself still in bed with them.

"What did you just say?" she whispered. She looked frightened.

"I don't know," I said groggily. "I was dreaming."

Desmond leaned up on one arm. "What is it?" he asked.

"Brandon just said the name we do not say," she replied.

"That's not possible," he said.

Kyra cradled my face in her cool hands, staring into my eyes. "Tell me your dream," she demanded. "Quickly, while it is still fresh."

I did as she requested, omitting the fact I'd had the dream twice and my inhabiting first his and then her body. When I was finished, she laid her head against Desmond's shoulder and he put his arms around her.

"Get dressed," Desmond said. "I'll make us some mulled wine."

I sat up, pulled my legs over the side of the bed, and maneuvered myself onto my chair. My erection was gone; my body below the waist was no more under my control than when I'd lain down. I wheeled myself to my discarded shirt and pulled it on, nervous again but trying not to let it show.

Desmond ignited a burner on the stove. Kyra sank to her knees before me.

"This happens sometimes, Brandon," she said. "An unfortunate effect that can come from my tears. In the past, when I have healed others, they have had dreams about Desmond and me. Those who receive the dreams are connecting to us on a very deep level. They have flashes of how we came to be together. But they are incomplete moments that we can explain away. Most times the dreamers will just explain them away for themselves."

"Then why are you telling me this?" I asked. "Why aren't you just explaining it away?"

I held back tears, fearing what she might say next.

"Because you know what they only imagined, Brandon. You saw what we keep in the closet, and the wounds on my back. You do not suspect, you *know*."

"You're an angel," I said.

"No," she said. "I am not. I am just a little bit closer to being one than you are."

Desmond stepped over and laid a hand gently on Kyra's shoulder.

"Don't say any more," he told her softly. "Brandon doesn't need to hear it."

"Yes, he does," she responded. "No one has ever brought that name from our dream. It comes with purpose. I have felt the madness myself. If we do not tell him, he is going to end up in a mental institution. I am not healing him just to condemn him to that."

Now I was truly alarmed. Desmond was not pleased, though I was sure he could not deny her.

"Come into the kitchen and we'll discuss it," he said.

We moved to the table. Desmond handed us each a steaming mug of the mulled wine. I couldn't have been less interested in drinking it.

"Please, have some," Kyra said softly. "The wine will make this easier for you."

The welcome warmth of the alcohol rushed through me with the first sip.

"Please continue, Kyra," I said. "If you're not an angel, what are you?"

"Are you sure you want to hear this, Brandon?" Desmond responded. "It's not easy to tell, and it's likely to change how you view the world."

"Knowing the two of you has already done that," I said.

"Consider carefully," he added. "We've never shared our story with anyone before. It's possible that what you hear could put you in danger, though I hope that won't be the case once we've healed you and left Los Angeles forever."

I was torn—and frightened. What good would knowing their story do me? Did I really need the information if I was never going to see them again? What kind of danger could there be? Maybe Desmond was just trying to protect Kyra, who was obviously worried. But I'd come this far, and knew I'd regret it if I didn't seize this opportunity, whatever the cost.

"I'd really like to hear it," I said.

"All right," he said, turning to Kyra. "Which of us should tell him?"

"You, my love," she replied. "My English is not good enough, and I long to hear you remember it."

CHAPTER 11

DESMOND'S TALE

I'm going to leave out some details regarding exact locations, and some of the more private moments, but I'll give you the best recounting I can.

I'm a mountaineer by trade. I've been climbing since I was a kid. My dad was a climber and so was my grandfather—I guess you could say it was in our blood. My grandmother used to tease us that our side of the family descended from mountain goats.

I don't actually remember my first climb. According to my family, I somehow made it up and out of my crib before I was even a year old. When I was seven, I successfully scaled the side of the three-story house where I grew up without any gear, and broke my leg on the way down. I was arrested for rappelling down the side of my junior high school when I was thirteen. By seventeen I'd conquered every Class Seven hunk of rock in North America. My dad and I climbed Mount McKinley on a Christmas vacation in Alaska, during one of the coldest winters on record. On my spring break we did Citlaltépetl and Iztacci-huatl in Mexico. When a piton I was sure had struck home gave way, Dad saved my life by hoisting me to safety at the end of a rope I hadn't secured correctly. I took a break for a while, but by nineteen I was certified and got right back out there, earning money as an instructor and traveling the world, tackling all the great climbs in succession: Elbrus in Russia, Khüiten in Mongolia, Kilimanjaro in Tanzania, the Matterhorn in Switzerland, K2 (where I got my first, near-fatal dose of altitude sickness), and finally Everest. My dad and grandfather came along on that expedition. Both of them reached the summit well before me. I think it was the proudest moment we ever shared—three generations of my family together atop the world's highest peak.

Shortly after my twenty-third birthday, my grandfather died suddenly from a heart attack. It devastated my dad and me. At the funeral, we decided to make a climb in his honor, one that was just beyond our comfort zone, which seemed fitting. It took weeks to select a summit, then several months of planning, guide selection, visa applications, and the like. Dad and I trained together vigorously. We took extra care to choose the perfect gear, sparing no expense. I packed several treasured tools from my grandfather's kit as well as his prided lucky parka.

I won't name the summit. Suffice to say it's in the Himalayas and had never been successfully navigated during the winter. When the time came to leave, the weather forecasts were not favorable. Mom wasn't happy about it, aware that we'd be at substantial risk. But she understood our need to do it. She'd known what she was getting into when she married Dad. My girlfriend at the time was a bit less understanding. We broke up a few weeks before the trip.

Everything started off well. The sky was clear when we reached northern Pakistan. We were met by our Sherpa guides, who'd arrived a day earlier from Nepal. One of them had been with us on Everest and knew our strengths and weaknesses. We paid them half their rate in advance. They would guide us three-quarters of the way up and assist in the creation of our base camps, then wait while we made the climb to the summit.

The four of us trekked for the better part of a day into the foothills. We slept the first evening in a tiny mountain village populated by natives who traded with us for fresh food supplies.

They were fascinated by our modern clothes and white faces. Dad had brought along a small box of Crayola crayons he gave to one of the village kids, who made a nuisance of himself until we allowed him to "assist us" by finding dinner and guarding our bags. He procured us side-by-side outdoor baths heated by burning yak dung, with a breathtaking view of the mountains. That kid loved those crayons.

The first day out was mostly hiking. We wormed our way up existing routes pretty much nonstop until nightfall, and built our first camp. The weather was holding, and we were enthusiastic it would stay that way. We drank bourbon by a small fire to keep warm, and reviewed our plans. The Sherpas were concerned with the route we'd chosen, which had never successfully been completed. They'd been present for several failed attempts, the majority of which ended with fatalities. But it was a record we'd set out to accomplish, despite the risks. The elder guide, who knew us well, vouched to his companion that we were extremely cautious climbers who would turn back immediately if conditions warranted.

The second day we ascended to just above ten thousand feet. It snowed a little—not enough to cause alarm, but it slowed us down. Later that evening the winds began howling and the temperatures plummeted. We lay in our tents listening to the radio forecast. A storm warning was in place for the next forty-eight hours. Neither dad nor I voiced our concerns, but I'll admit I had difficulty falling asleep that night.

The following morning the sun was shining. We took it as a sign from Granddad that he had things under control, and decided to continue on.

At fifteen thousand feet we began to walk on water—that is, we hiked paths marked as waterways during the summer that were now frozen over. We ascended for nine hours, some of the toughest climbing I'd ever done. By the time we reached the plateau we'd selected for our first base camp, dark clouds were gathering in the east. Setting up took well into the night. Light snow was falling by the time we surrendered to exhausted sleep. Come morning we were covered; we had to dig ourselves out. It's always a little scary when you wake to find your shelter interred. You can't tell at first how deep you're buried. But it wasn't that deep and the sun was blazing, so again we decided to push upward.

We left the requisite portion of supplies at base camp one and set out, climbing ten hours that day. Just about all of it was icy rock. The only sounds to be heard were the cracks of our picks and the pounding of our hammers on pitons, accompanied by our heavy breathing and determined grunts. Dad and I were tied together as one team, the Sherpas as another. Each of us had several slips, but none resulted in injury. We set our second base camp under cloudless skies at twenty thousand feet, on a westward-facing ridge in the shadow of the summit. It seemed the safest plateau we could find or reach easily—any other prospective site would have added an extra day to the climb—although if it snowed the next day it would be harder to clear things out. With camp two set, the Sherpas' work was basically done for now. They would remain there while Dad and I continued on our own, and wait for our return.

It was cold as hell the next morning, and the altitude was beginning to get to me. But Granddad's bargain with the sun still held. We decided to go for the summit. Dad filled a small flask with bourbon and gave the rest of the bottle to the grateful Sherpas. They cooked us a departing meal of hearty yak stew and said prayers over us in their native tongue for our swift journey and safe return. Placing his hands on my shoulders, Dad asked me to set aside my pride and be sure I was ready for the hard part. It would be a grueling climb to the summit, at least twelve to thirteen hours, with only our skills, determination, and God's grace to sustain us. I told him I was ready.

We checked and rechecked our equipment, stowing water and jerky in places we could access easily. We harnessed ourselves, engaged our safety ropes, and dug our boots in to begin the final ascent, taking the Sherpas' advice and choosing the mountain face that remained in the shadow of the summit.

The first five hours were easy going for me. I remember watching my father pick and grab and choose his footholds with care. His breathing had grown labored; I wondered if this would be his last major climb. He wasn't as young as he used to be, and no one had ever aged as slowly as my grandfather.

The sixth hour presented an unforeseeable difficulty: to clear an overhang of ice that could not be avoided required us to proceed nearly horizontally for some distance. It was one of the most difficult maneuvers either of us had ever made. We had to keep close and assist each other. When we finally cleared it, we sat on the upper ledge and took a breather to fill up on water and eat jerky. Base camp two was by then a couple thousand feet below us. We snapped several photos of each other, and some amazing panoramic shots of the view. We were nearly on top of the world again, as we'd been with my grandfather on Everest. We felt his absence along with a sense of accomplishment.

The sun was still full, but we saw dark clouds in the distance. At the rate we were going we could reach the summit before sunset. We decided we could handle a little rain or snow as long as the wind stayed calm. About an hour later we were still progressing nicely, slow and steady, when snow began to fall lightly. Two hours later the winds picked up dramatically.

We began to regret our decision, but it was too late to turn back. We looked around for emergency shelter, a cave or a crevasse to enter and bolt into in case of emergency. There were no such havens in sight. So we continued going higher, the wind buffeting our lines as we struck our pitons with greater urgency, gathered slack on our ropes with more care, made every movement count as best as we could.

That's when the hailstorm began, and with it my first twinge of panic. The wind doubled in intensity, raining chunks of ice the size of golf balls down on us. Our clothing and goggles protected us, but visibility was reduced to zero. We were forced to employ safety measures that left us dangling side by side, relying on our training and store-bought ropes as the wind and ice had their way with us.

Suddenly, the hail subsided. The winds died down. Sunlight streamed on us. Just when we thought the worst was over, we heard the first grumblings from above, and knew we were in serious trouble.

I lowered my goggles and looked up to see a giant sheet of ice and snow break away from the mountain and begin its rapid descent. It would reach us in minutes; there was no way to avoid it. I looked down. The shelf where we'd sat only hours before broke away and collapsed toward base camp two. I prayed the Sherpas had seen it in time to tie off or find cover, but doubted it.

Dad reached over and calmly took my hand. It was impossible to speak in the thunderous din. He smiled, not a hint of fear in his eyes. The avalanche blasted us, snapping the ropes and sweeping me away in cold, wet, suffocating, blinding whiteness.

I guess you could say that the fact I survived the avalanche was the first miracle I experienced. I was buried God knows how deep in ice and snow, aware enough to know I had stopped falling. I couldn't see. I tasted blood in my mouth. Neither my arms nor my legs worked. I assumed they were broken. Only the fingers on my left hand were capable of movement. I wriggled them against the packed wet snow, and knew I could never dig myself free. I resigned myself to the fact I was going to die.

Who knows how long I lay there entombed, wracked with pain? Time stopped. The cold numbed everything save for a dull throb in my temples. At some point I heard a distant sound like clawing, coming, it seemed, from above me. Was I imagining it? I dared myself to believe it was someone somehow digging me out. Then light stung my eyes and strong hands raised me up. I could barely feel their touch. I wanted to thank them, but was incapable of speech. Three impossibly tall men began to carry me. They appeared to have large, folded wings attached to their bare backs. It occurred to me that my rescue was a dying delusion.

Then I passed out.

I woke to pain. My bones ached. My skin felt dead in some places, severely burned in others. There was light from a fire burning in a small stone hearth near where I lay, on a bed dressed with animal hides. A woman of indeterminate age sat beside me, dabbing my brow with a wet, sweet-smelling poultice. She was bare-chested, with kind eyes, long translucent gray-white hair ... and wings.

"Ben-Noach," she said softly, pointing at me. Then she indicated herself and said, "Ruhamah."

"Ruhamah," I whispered, acknowledging her name.

This pleased her considerably.

During the following days, Ruhamah cared for me, fed me, cleaned me, and was constantly nearby. Many others visited our stone structure, all tall, winged, bare-chested like Ruhamah, and dressed like her in crude, handmade clothes. All of them, including the men, had unusually long hair. They'd stare at me from the doorway with wonder, calling me Ben-Noach, and sometimes say things I could not understand in their throaty language. I told them my real name on several occasions, but they never acknowledged or used it.

One day I woke to find the most beautiful creature I have ever laid eyes on sitting by my bedside opposite Ruhamah. Of course, I mean Kyra. She'd been given the task of learning about me.

Our language lessons were slow going at first, partly because I couldn't use my hands to gesture. But Kyra was very good using hers. And she learned fast, absorbing my words like a sponge.

The first word I taught her was my name. I was grateful

when she began to use it, because it restored a small part of my identity. She told me her name. Her language sounded vaguely like Hebrew.

I learned that Ruhamah was her mother, and that Kyra was one of the few in the tribe who knew all the words in their Great Book. As soon as possible I managed to convey to her that my father had also fallen during the avalanche, and I would be grateful if her tribesmen would search for him. She left to communicate this to her people immediately, then came back and assured me it was being done.

One of the first things she taught me was the word for "forbidden," tapping her fingers to her lips and shaking her head. The word would come up a lot during our lessons. By means of a sort of dance she performed at my bedside, I came to know who Kyra and her people were. She used the word "Yahweh" and indicated that He lived above us somewhere. I knew the name from the Old Testament. I nodded that I understood, which visibly pleased Kyra, and taught her the corresponding word, "God." We used that as a substitute. She twined her thumbs together and spread her hands with a wing-flapping motion above her head.

"Angel," I said, reinforcing my understanding by tipping my chin, first to indicate her, then Ruhamah, who sat listening by the fire. Kyra shook her head and pointed back to me.

"I'm not an angel," I said. "I'm a man."

She repeated the words "man" and "not an angel" several times. Then her face lit up. She began using gestures I understood to mean "children" in relation to God and angels.

"Angels are the children of God?" I hazarded.

She thought about what I had said and how I had said it, and repeated it several times. Then she indicated herself and her mother.

"Not an angel," she explained. *"Nepha."*

"Nepha," I echoed, glancing from her to Ruhamah and back. "You are the children of angels."

Kyra made the wing-flapping gesture, pointed to me, and made a new gesture: both hands gripped tightly together, trying to pull apart. It took me a moment to understand that she meant "union." Then it dawned on me she meant "sexual union." I taught her the term. She said it aloud. I watched fascinated as she put them together.

"Nepha are ... forbidden children ... of angels in sexual union with ..." She pointed to me.

"With men," I said.

Kyra smiled. She was telling me she and her people were half-angels, the product of sex between angels and men.

That ended our lesson for the day. I was taking a long time to mend, and needed a lot of sleep. Ruhamah's poultices soothed me, but I continued to experience a low level of pain coupled with mounting frustration at my lack of mobility.

Kyra and I were alone when she next visited, Ruhamah having been summoned by Azareal, the tribe's leader and eldest living Nepha. I asked Kyra to tell me more about her people.

I came to understand that Nepha originally came from the union of male angels and human females. A human male could not sire a Nepha with a female angel. The first Nepha had been born a very long time ago—how long, they couldn't say. The Nepha had no concept of years. They kept track of their history by how many generations separated them from the angels who initially fathered them. (Obviously they could reproduce among themselves.) Ruhamah was six generations "separated from grace," the term we agreed on for "related to angels." Neither Kyra nor her mother, nor any Nepha who now lived except Azareal, had ever seen a real angel. Azareal had told the tribe he remembered being brought here by the angels, along with several other Nepha children, and soon after abandoned forever; that he was the last of the first generation separated from grace who still lived. The tribe believed him.

According to their Great Book and commonly held belief, that was just before the Great Flood—which, if it really happened, was more than four thousand years ago. Doubtful as that seemed, I didn't argue with Kyra. I asked her to explain why the angels had abandoned the Nepha. She communicated to me that the angels wished to protect their children from the Great Flood, and this would be the only safe place when God sent the rain to punish and destroy men.

"I am a man," I reminded her. "God did not destroy my people."

"You are Ben-Noach."

She mimed a large boat on water. I realized she must mean Noah's Ark.

"You're calling me a Son of Noah."

"Yes," she said emphatically. "Son ... of ... Noah. Ben-Noach."

Which, if you believed in the Flood, was technically true. Noah's family were the only people who survived it; therefore, every human being now alive would be descended from Noah.

I couldn't help but think of my real father, and my hope that he had somehow survived the avalanche. I asked Kyra if there was any word about him.

"He was not found," she said.

I burst into tears.

Kyra seemed astonished when she saw this. Thinking that she did not understand why I was crying, I explained that it was because I had to accept that my father was dead. She continued to look bewildered.

"Tears come when people we love are in danger," I said, hoping she would understand. "Or sometimes when we are very happy or in love. I cried when my grandfather died."

Her response was so unexpected it shocked me.

"Nepha males cannot shed tears," she said.

"Is it forbidden?"

"Their bodies cannot create them."

"Can Nepha women cry?"

"Only after sexual union. Our mates break our hearts with joy, and our tears heal the wounds of our mates."

Her brow furrowed. Suddenly she looked terribly sad.

"Are you unhappy, Kyra?"

She seemed to silently debate with herself. Finally, she spoke.

"You are dying, Desmond. My mother hides the pain away from you, but the signs are clear. It saddens me."

Somehow I wasn't completely surprised. That explained why I was still bedbound, though it seemed to me that I wasn't as badly off as when I'd first revived and found myself in this extraordinary situation.

I lay silent as Kyra explained the extent of my injuries and lamented that Ruhamah's poultice was merely numbing my wounds. It could not heal me. Kyra had asked permission to select a Nepha woman to weep over me and save my life, but Azareal had forbidden it. He was certain I was sent to spy on them. Kyra was assigned to learn from me the intentions of the Sons of Noah, our number, and the whereabouts of our tribe, before allowing me to die. Having spent time with me, she no longer considered his belief sound. Knowing that none of her people would defy Azareal, she had considered performing the healing herself, but if she did, she would be disobeying her betrothed for all the tribe to see.

Azareal always had four wives, chosen from among the youngest and most beautiful of their kind. One of them, Esanna, had passed recently by her own hand, an unforgivable sin. Her name would be forgotten and stricken from the Book of Life. Azareal had selected Kyra to succeed her, a great honor. Their marriage was set for the start of the coming harvest. But she had no desire to marry him. Azareal was often cruel to her in private, and more than once had severely wounded her. She feared the abuse would grow worse once she was his. She believed that he may have driven Esanna to kill herself.

All this Kyra confided to me in whispers. She dared not speak of it to any of her own people, not even Ruhamah. We were alone, and my language offered her privacy from anyone who might be eavesdropping. She felt it was very unfair that I should die when my salvation was so simply accomplished. Not saving me was an affront to God's holy commandment: Thou shalt not murder. Azareal was acting as if he were above God's law, and by preventing Kyra from saving me he would condemn her in God's eyes. He would, in effect, be condemning all the Nepha.

Azareal didn't see it that way. He proclaimed that my death was in the hands of God, because the Nepha were forbidden to interfere in the lives of men.

Kyra was determined to save me.

She decided to seek her mother's guidance. She hoped Ruhamah, the most renowned healer in the tribe, might be sympathetic to my plight. Fearing that Azareal would retaliate if Kyra wept on my behalf, Ruhamah offered an alternative: the Sacred Tree of Life. The fruit was forbidden to the Nepha, but Ruhamah believed it could heal me.

At this point, I must admit I wondered if any of this was real, or if in fact I was still buried in ice and snow and these were delusions of my dying mind. Men and women with wings surviving undiscovered since the time of Noah, who believed they'd descended from angels? My life to be determined by a piece of fruit from a magic tree, or a woman crying on me? Surely I'd gone insane. But some inner voice urged me to keep going, to play out the dream and see where it led me. Unless I had died and this was hell, time was running out.

Kyra and I struck on a plan and put it into action.

Kyra left to bring a message to Azareal: I would reveal to him all I knew about the Sons of Noah—how we survived the Flood, what happened to the angels, how many of us there were now, where we lived—but only in public, in the presence of all the Nepha.

While we waited nervously for Kyra's return, Ruhamah roughly pressed brown nettles against my fingertips, my palms, my toes, and the balls of my feet. They stung mightily. Was this some form of acupuncture meant to strengthen me? She was mopping my brow with the poultice when two male Nepha arrived. They spoke harsh words to Ruhamah, then lifted me unceremoniously from the bed and carried me, naked, from the chamber.

Outside for the first time in days, I felt the cold in my eyes, my nostrils, and against my skin as I drank in my surroundings. The sky above seemed murky, impenetrable, a half-light. In the distance, I could just make out a jagged wall of ice, sloping upward, and wondered where on Earth I was.

The path we took was paved with flat, crafted stones; I saw the occasional patch of fallen snow. Woods surrounded us, so wherever I'd landed was below the timberline. I heard water rushing and caught sight of a stream in the distance.

They brought me to the village square, which stood among simple stone structures, a few as tall as five or six stories. There seemed to be dozens of them, many with crude metal chimneys. At the center of the square a giant fig tree towered upward. It looked like it might indeed be thousands of years old, the roots great gray appendages themselves like tree trunks jutting from the ground, interspersed by lush flowers of indescribable color and fragrance. From its branches hung the fruit that Kyra's mother believed might heal me.

About ten yards away from the tree was a crude stone platform set before a wall of rock with ominous chains bolted into it. On the platform Kyra stood between two brutish-looking male Nepha, with the tribe congregating beneath them, including several Nepha children. They all turned as my two abductors roughly carried my limp body forward through the crowd, my arms slung across their shoulders, and held me aloft in front of the platform.

The eyes of all the Nepha were on me, the first man they'd ever seen, and I was making a terrible show: wingless, hairy as a wild beast, bruised and battered, unable to stand on my own power. The air quivered with expectation.

The stillness was broken by a thunderous sound above us like waves crashing on a beach or millions of leaves stirring against a huge wind, but rhythmic, pulsating. It grew louder. Everyone looked up.

A figure, its vast black wings thrashing, swooped down and hovered before settling onto the platform between Kyra and her companions and contracting his wings. Not only was he bigger than all the other Nepha, his features were sharper, his skin pale, his hair and eyes black.

The assembled Nepha bowed from the waist, murmuring, "Azareal, Azareal." He acknowledged their homage with a nod, and stared at me. He'd made quite an entrance for my benefit.

"Son of Noah," he said coldly, his eyes burning into me, "you have asked to be heard, and I shall hear you. Speak falsely and I shall know it."

Kyra translated, to make sure I understood what was being said.

"Great Azareal, leader of the Nepha, I thank you," I responded, speaking slowly so that Kyra could follow. "I fell among your people by accident. I do not come to spy on you. No other Sons of Noah know you are here. I swear to God I will not tell them."

Somehow I knew that if I lied, not only Azareal, but all the Nepha, would know in an instant. Conversely, I prayed that they knew I was speaking the truth.

"Where is your tribe? How far from here? Who is their leader?"

"You have been here a very long time," I said. "My tribe is now many separate tribes. They are spread out across the world. Few live close to you. They speak many tongues, and have no common leader."

"What is your number? How many Sons of Noah are spread across the world?"

Archeologists estimate that before the Flood the human population ranged somewhere between 100 and 500 million. How did I tell the leader of fewer than a hundred Nepha that there were now several billion people on Earth, much less that we were capable of annihilating his little tribe in moments? He believed all of Mankind save a handful had perished long ago.

"God has blessed us with union," I said. "The sons and daughters of Noah have been fruitful. Our number is far greater now, at least ten times what it was before the Great Flood."

This sent a clamor through the Nepha. Even Azareal and Kyra seemed stunned.

"What about the angels? What part do they play in the world?"

"They have been gone as long as you have, Great Azareal. When I saw your people, I believed the Nepha were angels."

I let that sink in for a moment, then lowered my head in supplication.

"Great Azareal, I beg that you show me mercy. Grant me the fruit of the Sacred Tree, so that I might live on to consult you further about the Sons of Noah."

I kept my head down as Kyra translated, not daring to look up, hoping that the chance for him to learn more about my kind might save me. I was also making clear to the assembled Nepha that my death would be Azareal's choice, should he deny me the fruit.

Azareal was too clever for such tactics.

"The Nepha are forbidden to touch the fruit of the Sacred Tree. We are also forbidden to interfere in the lives of men," he responded with a terrifying smile.

"Then I ask that you not interfere, and let God decide my fate. As a Son of Noah chosen by God to survive the Great Flood, I beg that you allow me to try to take the fruit myself."

I had placed him in a terrible position. If he denied my request, he would be usurping God's power in the eyes of his flock. On the other hand, he knew that my reaching the tree, much less claiming the fruit, was next to impossible. I didn't believe I could make it unaided, but he had left me no other course of action. I kept my head bowed, sure that Azareal cursed me for flouting his will.

After what seemed like an interminable pause, he smiled at me grimly.

"Very well, Son of Noah, try to reach the fruit. We will not interfere."

He flicked his hand to the two Nepha who held me aloft. They released my arms. I crumpled to the ground at their feet. The assembled Nepha parted to clear a path to the tree. The base was approximately thirty feet away, the lowest branch bearing fruit at least ten feet off the ground. Naked, on my belly, I began my slow, impossible crawl.

I knew that my left hand worked but doubted that any other parts of my body would. The ground beneath me was covered with grass. I reached out and dug my left hand into the earth, got a firm hold, and pulled, dragging myself several inches forward. In this manner, I moved along the ground at a slug's pace, straining every muscle in my arm, blocking out the pain, desperate to use my feet, which had begun to tingle, presumably due to Ruhamah's crude acupuncture. If I could get my feet working, even one foot, intermittently, in tandem with my good hand, I could propel rather than drag myself. As I slid along on my belly, certain muscles I attribute to climbing began to respond by memory, and, if I ignored the pain, did their work reflexively, helping me forward. Then the toes of both feet began to burn. I flexed them, and felt a modicum of control over my right foot. Using my left hand to grip and pull, and right foot to dig and push, after what seemed like an hour I reached the first of the tree's great roots. It scaled several feet up the side of the trunk. I inched my dead weight along the side, hardly noticing the fragrance of the lush flowers I crushed.

Finally, I reached the massive tree trunk. I observed the first handhold above me that I needed to make, if I could somehow summon the strength to raise myself. I tried several times and failed. I simply could not raise my hand high enough to secure a grip. I looked up and saw a single fig amid the leaves, hanging low on a bent branch, as if God were teasing me. I tried again, stretching out my hand, and dropped it, exhausted. I was ready to give up.

It was as if I heard Azareal's mocking laughter in my head, willing it so. I was completely tapped out. My fingers failed to respond to any attempt to raise them. I closed my eyes and accepted, with a kind of relief, the fact that it was over.

And then I heard singing. The air was filled with wondrous melody.

It was the Nepha.

The song gained in volume as one by one they joined in, raising their beatific voices, it seemed, to Heaven. Warmth enveloped me, penetrating every pore in my body, saturating my bones and pervading me with resolve—and the strength I needed to raise my hand. I started to climb. It was a terrible struggle, but finally the fruit was mine. Only then did the singing stop.

I don't remember the climb at all, or eating the fruit. Kyra told me about it afterward. How the Nepha, when they saw I was giving up, could not contain themselves, and caught up in a religious fervor, one by one began to sing for me. All except Azareal. The next thing I remember is waking up in bed exhausted with Ruhamah sitting beside me. Every muscle in my body burned, but I knew I was healed. Ruhamah gave me cool water to drink, insisting I not get up, even though I felt I could. Through her long, difficult explanation, I came to understand that Azareal blamed Kyra for all that had happened. Furious, he'd dragged her away from the square by her arm. None of the Nepha had seen her since then. Ruhamah assured me that Azareal wouldn't hurt Kyra, but I didn't believe it. Concerned for her safety, despite Ruhamah's pleading, I got out of bed and dressed myself in the animal hide clothing she'd procured for me, intent on finding Kyra.

Two male Nepha blocked the door. They, or other Nepha, stood guard outside for several days while I was kept from public view in Ruhamah's quarters, until Azareal decided my fate. During this time I began a strenuous regimen of exercise to regain my strength, and voraciously ate everything given to me. I planned to climb back out of there as soon as I got the chance.

One morning Kyra arrived at the door, dressed in flowing robes. She had flowers in her hair and a faraway look in her eyes. Ruhamah kissed her daughter's cheeks and left us alone together. Though the guards remained watchful, they could not understand what we were saying. Kyra told me that she was very happy to see me up and about. I thanked her for all she had done to save my life. Then she informed me that she and Azareal had been married. She now belonged to him. I admit I was sad to hear it, but at that point I had no illusions about ever being with her myself. To me she was an angel, and I was merely a man. I just wanted to be allowed to return to my life and family.

Then she informed me that although my life would be spared, I was forbidden to leave. My presence had sparked a great debate among the Nepha. Upon hearing that the Sons of Noah had repopulated the world, many felt the Nepha should reveal their existence and demand their rightful place. Azareal reminded them that the angels had placed the Nepha in the Haven with a strict warning that leaving was forbidden; the angels would return to set them free at the Time of Judgment, which Azareal warned might soon be at hand. Azareal's word was law. But unrest was growing, and Kyra feared for my safety. She had come to tell me Azareal's plan. I was to remain there, publicly renounce the world of men, discontinue speaking my native language, abide by their laws, and agree to marry a Nepha of Azareal's choosing. Azareal wanted an answer now. If I refused, she was sure I would die by some unfortunate accident.

Having no choice, I agreed. Kyra knew I was lying. She

always knew. And when I asked her why she'd risked Azareal's wrath, risked death at his hand, she told me it was just to save my life—and we both knew she was lying, too.

So I was given my freedom, and assigned menial tasks like washing hides by the stream, herding llamas and goats, and working in the fields beside the Nepha. They grew used to my presence and were pleasant to me, though only Kyra and Ruhamah treated me as an equal. I came to realize that the days were shorter here. Could it be that we were *inside* the mountain, in some unbelievably massive cavern? That there were breaks in the unseen roof that allowed for a limited number of hours of diverted sunlight to filter through the constant haze hovering high above us? Or was the Haven some hidden valley? I might never know the answers to these questions if Azareal had his way.

I spent my days regaining my strength and observing the Nepha's storehouse of crude tools for those that might aid in my escape. At first I saw Kyra mostly at mealtimes. She sat in fourth position from Azareal at the head of the great communal table. I was in lowest position. Occasionally Kyra contrived to take walks with me. One day we had gone beyond the great waterfall that was the source of the Nepha's irrigation system, supplying fresh water and all kinds of fish to the village. I was telling Kyra about the small town where I grew up, about my dad and my grandfather, and how they would have marveled at this place. About our giant cities. Kyra confessed that she wished she could see them with me. Taking my hand, she brought her body close. I felt her heart beating fast in her chest. I took her beautiful face in my hands, leaned in close, and tenderly kissed her. She sighed as our lips touched; her arms closed tightly around my back, molding her to me. I closed my eyes, savoring the taste of her mouth and her sweet smell. Her shoulders trembled. It seemed as if my feet left the ground, and we were floating on air. I opened my eyes, and realized that we were. Kyra's wings were in gentle motion behind her; she had literally lifted us up several feet.

She smiled and propelled us to the edge of the treetops, low enough that we wouldn't be observed, but high enough for me to see the Haven in all its splendor.

The great waterfall winding down to a gentle stream through the woods and along the banks of the fields up to the meadow. The path of stone, I now saw, was a perfect spiral threading inward to the village square with its charming stone dwellings, the chimneys billowing thin plumes of smoke. In the distance, the glistening slopes of ice ascended skyward like an overturned funnel. This gorgeous, fertile valley was indeed a cavern deep inside the mountain—undiscovered and untouched by modern man.

Kyra kissed me as we hovered. Desire coursed through my body. We twined our legs together and floated for what seemed an eternity. It was almost sad, coming back down to Earth. She landed us so gently I forgot to find my footing and stumbled. How we laughed at my clumsiness!

I won't detail our intimacies on future walks, nor the improprieties that occurred behind the closed doors of Ruhamah's quarters on nights when Kyra had supposedly come to visit her. Finally, a day arrived when Kyra's vows were broken.

That's what you dreamed, isn't it, Brandon? The two of us in the tall grasses on the far outskirts of the village. If you saw that, you know it was as inevitable as it was remarkable. You also know why I won't defile the memory by describing it. Still, I will tell you this: Kyra brought me closer to God than I had ever dared dream possible, and does so to this day. Unfortunately, you were not the only witness. Azareal had followed us, and as you now know cast his great winged shadow over our adulterous union.

Terrified, we fled to Ruhamah's house and told her what had happened. She spoke harshly to Kyra, saying that I must escape quickly, before Azareal came to tear me apart. She barred the door with a heavy plank, then moved to a small wooden cabinet beside the stone hearth and retrieved the clothes I was wearing on my arrival. Just then the door was battered in, the plank splintering like balsa wood. Two of Azareal's loyal Nepha stormed into the cabin and tore Kyra from my arms.

Ruhamah and I followed helplessly as they dragged her, struggling, to the village square where a crowd of Nepha was gathering, drawn by Kyra's screams. Azareal descended onto the stone platform, his face a mask of fury, and with a glance to his Nepha indicated the chains. The Nepha dragged Kyra onto the platform and bound her with her back exposed to the crowd, her face and stomach pressed hard against the stone to which her wrists and ankles were clamped.

Two other Nepha seized me, wrestling me onto the platform and forcing me to my knees. Azareal hammered my face and stomach with shattering punches, knocking the wind out of me. I spat blood at his feet. As I tried vainly to break free from the Nepha who held me, he turned toward Kyra and extended his right hand sideways. Another of his Nepha placed in it a huge, leather-handled, jaggedly notched bone: a primitive saw. Azareal held it above his head, screamed several words I could not understand, and savagely hacked off Kyra's wings. I'm sure he wanted to go further, to murder us both, but the other Nepha crowded in to stop him. Kyra was unchained, and both of us were carried to Ruhamah's quarters. Kyra was laid in the bed where I had slept. I sat in Ruhamah's chair and watched her tend to Kyra's wounds with salves and poultices. I could tell she'd done this service before, but this was her daughter who'd been mutilated. I ached for her and for Kyra, knowing it was all my fault.

Desmond paused, clearly shaken—as was I.

"It is all right, my love," Kyra whispered, grasping his hand. "I am all right. He made me closer to you. I could not be here with you like this if he had not done it. It was not your fault. I wanted you. I love you with all of my heart and soul. I would make the same decision again if I could."

The lovers shared a look that will haunt me forever.

"Now tell Brandon the rest, my love."

Desmond kept Kyra's hand in his as he continued his story.

Ruhamah shared my fear that we would be murdered out of view if Azareal could somehow arrange it. She begged me to go immediately and take Kyra with me. I was more than happy to oblige her. But looking at Kyra's wounds, seeing her writhe and moan in agony, I couldn't imagine how she might even stand, much less leave with me.

Then Ruhamah opened her palm, revealing three ripe figs from the Sacred Tree. I assumed she stole them during the commotion that followed the abomination in the square. She had sinned for her daughter, and I would not let it be in vain. Ruhamah handed me two of the figs, then sat beside Kyra and force-fed the third to her. Once she swallowed it, Kyra began to calm almost immediately.

Ruhamah then handed me my old clothes, which she had cleaned and mended. I dressed quickly in my thermals, pocketed the figs in my cargo pants, laced up my steel-spiked boots, and zipped myself into my grandfather's parka. Meanwhile, Ruhamah sat Kyra up and spoke to her as she bandaged her wounds. Kyra seemed completely alert now, as if the pain were already under control. Ruhamah helped Kyra dress from head to toe in animal hides, with boots that looked like Eskimo mukluks. By then Kyra was standing on her own power. She retrieved her flute from where it hung on the wall, and asked if I would carry it for her. Ruhamah gave me dried meats I shoved into my pockets. Then she and Kyra embraced and spoke softly to each other.

Kyra said something that Ruhamah objected to strongly. Kyra persisted. Finally, Ruhamah acquiesced. She fetched a large yak-skin sack resembling a backpack and left us.

"I sent her for my wings," Kyra told me. "They are mine, and I will not depart without them."

When Ruhamah returned, I reached to take the now-bulging sack from her. Kyra pushed my hand away and slung it across her back. Mother and daughter said their goodbyes, knowing they were likely to be final. Then Kyra was ready to go.

We climbed through Ruhamah's rear window as night was falling and dropped low beneath shrubbery. There were no Nepha to be seen. We picked our path carefully through the trees with quiet steps, neither of us saying a word until we were well out of sight of the village. A feeling of sadness washed over me for Kyra, as we turned back for one final glimpse of the primitive stone buildings; the only home Kyra had ever known, where she was no longer welcome.

We quickened our pace along the stream, several yards off from the stone walkway that marked the village entrance, using trees to hide our progress should we be pursued from behind or above. Soon we were moving along a small ravine. The ground grew slick beneath us. Whenever one of us slipped, which grew more and more frequent, we held hands and practiced balancing each other as counterweights. Kyra led the way, having once been brought to the exact location where I had been found. Of course, she hadn't been on foot then, so a lot of our path now was literally just good guesswork on her part.

Eventually we reached the place where I had been entombed until the Nepha dug me out. On the side of the cliff, as far as I could see, were endless banks of glistening snow and ice, sloping dizzyingly upward. I thought of my dad. There were no signs of his body, and we had no means or time to search. We had to keep going, and I knew in my heart that was what he would have wanted me to do. Sensing my sadness, Kyra squeezed my hand to comfort me.

We began our ascent. The way up the slippery, ice-covered rocks was slow going, to say the least, and compounded by the fact that we were in darkness. I used my feet as a blind person might have done, feeling my way ahead, leading Kyra up the side of the cliff without incident. Then it began to grow steep. With no equipment or ropes, I needed to teach her how to use her hands in tandem with her feet to keep moving forward. As with our language lessons, she was a remarkably fast learner. Unaffected by the cold, she refused my gloves, convincing me that her survival would depend on mine.

Looking back, Brandon, I have to say the climb we made should have been impossible. It was a blur to both Kyra and me at the time, and remains so. We believe some benevolent force was watching over us. Or maybe the figs temporarily offered us strength and endurance beyond imagination. Perhaps it was both.

Eventually we found a plateau, where we rested for a time and ate our dried beef, peering downward at the land we were leaving. We couldn't see much through the haze. We had to keep moving. But the immediate issue was not the climb; it was the lack of destination. I sensed we were headed in the right direction, but could not detect the crevasse I knew I must have fallen through. Again, Kyra read my mind.

"What are you looking for?" she asked.

"An opening in the ice that may or may not still exist. There should be light coming through it."

"There," she said, pointing high above to our left. I followed her gaze along the cavern's edge and detected no difference. Trusting that she saw something I could not, we climbed in the direction she indicated. At times, I had to hoist her above me on my shoulders; she would find some grip to hold onto and in turn hoist me up. We could have slipped and died. As we made our final approach to the crevasse I knew must be there, it turned out she had been right.

It was a deep vertical shaft, about thirty feet long by twelve feet wide, with soft light filtering through; my entry point—and hopefully a safe exit—though getting ourselves up into it would not be easy. I decided the farthest edge would be our best bet. I taught Kyra how to ascend, and sent her up ahead of me. Luckily it was navigable, though it took some pretty grueling climbing to reach. We emerged along the mountainside to a sheer surface of soft snow that perhaps an expert could have skied down, though likely no one in their right mind would try it.

We sat holding each other on the ledge that the lip of the crevasse offered, catching our breath and gazing out at the Himalayas beneath the clear night sky.

"Shemesh?" Kyra said, pointing upward. *"Yare'ach?"* Words we had not used before.

I followed her gaze and realized she was asking if that big light up there was the sun or the moon, having never seen either.

"It's the moon," I responded.

She smiled radiantly.

"Wait till you see the sun."

CHAPTER 12

*D*esmond ended his story there, without detailing the rest of the journey down the mountain, saying only that though it had its perils it was a hundred times safer than the upward climb. He and Kyra had been on the run ever since they returned to civilization, lying low and keeping on the move. He looked exhausted—understandably. I was exhausted just from hearing about it.

"Perhaps someday you will tell the world our story, Brandon," Kyra said. "Then we will be remembered, and in hearing it people may find some small bit of healing."

"What do you think?" Desmond added with a wry laugh. "Enough to base a movie on?"

"More than enough," I said. "I'm sorry for what the two of you have been through."

"It has given us a purpose," Kyra said. "I know the question that burns inside you. I have no evidence that God exists. Unless you believe that my tears, and my wings, and the fruit of the Sacred Tree are proof enough. I am sorry."

Once again, Kyra had known what I was thinking.

"We have a busy day ahead," Desmond said, putting our

empty mugs in the sink. "We need to finish packing and load out."

"And have our third session?" I said.

"And have our third session," he confirmed. "Get some sleep, Brandon. We'll settle up the money for you and Bethany in the evening, and get you out of that wheelchair."

I rolled myself out of their apartment in a daze. Could the story I'd just heard be true? Would I really be able to walk again tomorrow night? I believed the answer to both questions was yes. I grabbed a bottle of Jägermeister from my freezer and poured myself a drink. I needed one if I had any hope of sleeping. Not bothering to get undressed, I pulled down the Murphy bed and maneuvered myself onto it.

I lay awake replaying Kyra and Desmond's story in my mind. What a terrible price they paid for their love, and Desmond had lost his father. I thought about Kyra. The terrible scars on her back. Her wings in the closet. Could there really be a tribe of half-human, half-angels living out there, somewhere, having survived undetected for millennia? Was there any record of them anywhere? I couldn't shake the question. Finally, I got out of bed and went to my computer.

Where to begin? I found several mountains in the Himalayas that could have matched Desmond's description, but all of them had been ascended. I searched for "Nepha" with various spellings. Nothing of interest came back. Then I included the words "Bible" and "flood," and "angel." And there it was, in Genesis 6:4:

The Nephilim were in the earth in those days, and also after that, when the sons of God came in unto the daughters of men, and they bare children to them: the same were the mighty men which were of old, the men of renown.

There was little more to be found in traditional Hebrew or Christian texts, but a site about the Dead Sea Scrolls had something from an ancient text called *The Book of Enoch*. Enoch was supposedly the great-grandfather of Noah. Though the Hebrews and Christians acknowledge his writings, they are not widely accepted as canon by either religion. Enoch speaks of angels who mated with the daughters of men, and how the interference of their offspring, the Nephilim, with the affairs of Mankind incited God's wrath and resulted in the Flood. That was all I could find on the subject. I shut down the computer and returned to bed.

And once again I was in the meadow. I quickened my pace when I heard Kyra in the clearing ahead. My heart filled with rage as I witnessed her and Desmond writhing in passion. I lunged skyward, beating my wings and soaring fast above them, intent on tearing the puny Son of Noah limb from limb. As I descended, Kyra began to shriek in ecstasy. I answered with a shriek of my own, plunging earthward. They looked up in horror.

I woke, sweating, realizing that in this dream I'd been seeing through Azareal's eyes. I couldn't dispel the feeling that Azareal was also seeing Kyra and Desmond—through my eyes—and that I had to warn them.

Suddenly there was insistent knocking at my door.

"Hang on, I'm coming," I yelled.

The knocking stopped. I struggled into my wheelchair, still half asleep and in yesterday's clothes. As I wheeled past the kitchen, I glanced at the clock. It was after noon. I opened the door as far as the security chain permitted.

A tall, gruff-looking man in his late thirties, wearing a tweed jacket, button-down shirt, and patent leather shoes, held up a badge with his right hand.

"My name's Detective Mendoza," he said. "May I come in?"

Did I actually have a choice? It was such a gray area where police were concerned in this town. And why was a detective at my door?

"Be my guest," I said, still groggy.

I closed the door to unhitch the chain, then opened it wide for him.

"Nice place," he said, stepping in and looking around.

"Pardon the mess. I just woke up."

He took in the uncapped bottle of Jäger on the counter beside my single glass.

"Out late last night? With friends maybe? Anything good?"

"I was at home," I responded. "May I ask what this is about?"

He ambled around the room for a few moments, silently examining the books and other objects on my shelves. If he was trying to unnerve me, he was succeeding. I needed to wake up fast.

"You're an actor, right?" he said. "I think I recognize you from something."

That explained him not asking my name.

"I've done some work you might have seen. Played a cop a couple of times."

"I thought so. Then you know how this works."

I did, for the most part, and was glad he wasn't reading me my rights.

"Were you by chance at Creative Artists Agency recently?"

That jolted me. What did any of this have to do with CAA? I told myself to stay on guard.

"I think I was there about a week ago," I answered. "I go to all the agencies—for auditions, readings, screenings. You know. Why do you ask?"

"Someone at the station has made some allegations about you involving an agent who works there. I'd appreciate it if you'd come down and help sort it out."

I told myself to be calm, at least until I learned what was going on. We both knew I had no real choice but to go with him.

Detective Mendoza's unmarked car pulled into the parking structure behind the West Hollywood police station on San Vincente Boulevard off Santa Monica. I let him struggle to unfold my chair from the trunk without offering any instruction. We had to go through a metal detector at the rear entrance, and I ended up getting patted down pretty thoroughly. I wasn't overly concerned with being brought in until we passed a small conference room and saw Margaret Tremaine's assistant, Emma, speaking to another plainclothes officer. What was she doing here?

Detective Mendoza pulled the chair away from the front of his desk in his small office to make room for my wheelchair, then seated himself and shuffled papers on the desktop. He opened a folder and leafed through it.

"I see that you were involved in a car accident about nine months back. DUI. The other driver died. Is that right?"

"Yeah," I said.

"I take it that's the reason you're in the wheelchair. Injury permanent?"

I nodded. He closed the folder.

"Okay. To the business at hand. Is it true that you told Ms. Pomeroy you work for *The Hollywood Reporter?*"

"Who's Ms. Pomeroy?"

"She's an assistant who works at CAA. You seemed to recognize her on the way in."

His phone rang.

"Homicide, Detective Mendoza," he answered. "I'm with him now. I'll come up when we're done."

"Homicide?" I asked. "Who's dead?"

"Who do you think?"

"I have no idea," I answered honestly, praying it wasn't Kyra or Desmond. "So why don't you tell me?"

He sat back in his chair and reached for a pen, which he tapped against the edge of his desk.

"Margaret Tremaine," he said. "The agent you spoke with at

CAA. Her body was found by a cleaning woman at the Mondrian Hotel, around 5:00 AM this morning, lying beside the swimming pool."

I allowed my shock to show on my face. To have died so soon after being healed.

"Did she drown?"

It was clear he hadn't been ready to answer that. Would have liked to have withheld that information a while longer, perhaps in hope of having me slip up, revealing I knew more than I should, but the question had been posed.

"No," he answered. "She apparently fell twelve floors from the top of the hotel. Every bone in her body was broken, including her neck."

I shook my head. I'd been to the Mondrian. It was pretty tall, an extravagant hideaway for the town's A-list. I pictured the glitzy Mediterranean-style pool deck on the ground floor, which offered a tremendous view of the city and was typically littered with half-naked models. It was hard to imagine Mrs. Tremaine's body lying there on the cement beside it.

"So she jumped?" I asked.

"I'm on the fence about that," Mendoza replied.

To be honest, I was right up there on the fence with him. Why kill yourself after all your prayers have been answered? The hairs went up on the back of my neck.

"You think someone might have pushed her?" I asked.

"On the fence about that, too," he answered, annoyingly tapping the pen some more. "We were ready to conclude her death a suicide, before Ms. Pomeroy showed up to volunteer her statement, making accusations against you."

"Accusations?" I said, my surprise genuine. "What exactly is Ms. Pomeroy accusing me of?"

Mendoza tapped the pen rapidly, searching my face, then offered, "Attempted blackmail."

"You're saying I'm a suspect?" There was a knot in my throat.

"That's what we're trying to determine."

"Why the hell would I try to blackmail Mrs. Tremaine?"

"I don't know, let's think about it. Seems your accident messed up your big break in that new hit series? Right after the pilot airs, you show up all agitated at CAA, lie your way in, say something so imperative on the phone that Mrs. Tremaine interrupts sick leave to come and meet you. We did some checking. You had a few bad auditions a while back. You're living on subsidies. You're bitter. Got yourself worked up and decided you wanted a top agent to represent you. Maybe she refused to take you on and that was the last straw. Ms. Pomeroy says that after you left Mrs. Tremaine was distressed. And now she's dead."

It was a stretch and we both knew it.

"That's ludicrous," I said. "You can't possibly believe that's a motive to try and blackmail someone, let alone kill anybody."

"Hey, this is Hollywood. I'm just considering possibilities. That's my job. So help me out. Tell me why you went to CAA."

I had to think fast. There was no way I could tell him the truth. But it might be safest to stick as close to the facts as possible without sounding like a madman. I needed Mendoza off my case, and to get back home for my last treatment.

"I went to pitch Mrs. Tremaine a story about a wandering preacher who heals people. You know, by laying his hands on them? I figured she'd be one of the few agents in town who would get it, seeing as how we were both handicapped. I think it's really good. But I knew I'd never get an appointment if I went through channels. I'm not known as a writer. So, I said I was from *The Hollywood Reporter*, because I didn't have an appointment. When Ms. Pomeroy told me Tremaine was on medical leave, I didn't believe her. I made up a story to convince her to see me. I admit it was extreme, but she agreed. Then I got worked up when I was pitching. And, yes, I was disappointed when she said no. But not enough to want to harm her."

Detective Mendoza looked at me intently while I spoke, then sat silently to see if I'd say anything else to implicate myself. When I didn't, he said, "Anything you want to add?"

"No."

"I think there's something you're not telling me," Mendoza said. "I'm going to hold you while I do some further checking."

"How long will it be?" I asked, hoping I didn't sound as panicked as I suddenly felt.

"We can hold you without charging you for twenty-four hours. Would you like to call someone?"

Who would I call? My parents? I hadn't spoken to them in months. Ray or Bethany? What could they do? There was no one.

"If I get a lawyer, how soon can I get out of here?" I asked.

"That I can't say, Brandon. I'm inclined to hold you as long as I can legally."

I thought about what being detained for twenty-four hours would mean. That Desmond and Kyra would be long gone, off on a boat somewhere, and with them any hope I had of ever walking again, or making love to a woman again, or leading a normal life again, thanks to that bitch, Emma, who would probably be sitting at a Starbucks by now, drinking a mochaccino, bobbing her ponytail and bravely recounting the story to one of her girlfriends. I couldn't really blame her. She believed she was doing the right thing. She must be freaking out over her boss's death.

And something broke inside me.

"Please, Detective. I don't have a lawyer and my parents can't afford one. Look at me. I'm not a flight risk. I have absolutely nothing to do with Mrs. Tremaine's death. I just pitched her a story and got carried away."

"If that's true, we'll be done with you when you leave. But for now, I'm going to hold you. I'm sorry, son."

I knew at that moment that the cure had slipped from my grasp. I wasn't being charged or arrested, but I may as well have been sentenced to life.

Detective Mendoza snapped a picture of me, then led me along a hallway past guards and through another metal detector to a table where I had to hand over my phone, my belt, and my shoelaces. After he left, I was locked in a graffiti-covered holding cell marked for the handicapped. It stunk of urine. By then it was late afternoon.

Alone in the cell, I brooded. How did Mrs. Tremaine die? Mendoza must believe she was murdered, or he wouldn't be holding me without evidence. Or could she have committed suicide? I found that hard to believe—unless she hadn't really been cured. With nothing else to do with my time, sure that one way or the other I was now condemned never to walk again, I tortured myself with possible scenarios. Could everything I believed be a scam perpetrated by Desmond and Kyra? What did I really know about them? How much of what I believed was simply the manifestation of my desire to be cured? I knew that Kyra was a beautiful foreigner. I'd broken into their apartment and found writing in old Hebrew and what appeared to be a pair of severed wings in the closet. Could they just be an elaborate prop? This was Los Angeles, after all, where such things are easy to obtain, and I'd only seen them in the dark. Had I been meant to find them? Provoked into breaking and entering by Desmond forbidding Kyra to see me, then "discovering" Mrs. Tremaine miraculously healed? Surely not. What about the scars on Kyra's back? Had she let her robe slip on purpose? It was only for a moment. Could what I saw have been clever makeup?

What about the treatments? I was on my stomach. I couldn't see what Kyra was doing to me after they made love. The first time nothing happened, but Mrs. Tremaine had prepped me for that. The second time there was the burning sensation. Had Kyra poured something on me, maybe some chemical? All I had to show for that, miraculous as it was, was a brief erection I could not repeat. There was no more evidence that the treatments were successful than there was proof that Mrs. Tremaine was ever really healed—which was what I had based my hopes on. What if she and Arthur were part of the scam? I had only her word that she'd paid Kyra and Desmond all that money, and now they had my ID—and Bethany's, too. Had their deal gone south? Was that why Mrs. Tremaine was dead?

Why would they go through all that trouble to scam me? It wouldn't be lucrative enough. Were they working the same scam on multiple people at once? Were Kyra and Desmond even their real names? Why add the perverted twist of me having to wait while they screwed, then rush into bed with them? And that story Desmond told me? Was it just a story? And how *had* Desmond and Kyra managed to climb that mountain without any equipment, and Kyra with no experience and carrying her wings in a sack, to boot? Was I so desperate to be healed, I'd fall for anything?

All I knew for certain was that Margaret Tremaine was dead. It was a good thing the police had taken my belt and shoelaces, for I was feeling utterly hopeless. I told myself to be sensible. Could Desmond and Kyra really be such good actors? The sequence of events was simply too unlikely. If they had to rely on that kind of thing for all their scams, they'd remain as poor as I was. And I had been with them almost all of last night. I refused to believe that they'd somehow gone out and done away with Mrs. Tremaine after I left their apartment. That was too crazy, even for my fevered imagination.

I must have nodded off. The next thing I remember is Detective Mendoza entering my cell.

"You're free to go, Brandon," he said. "We're letting you out early."

"Why?" I asked.

"You're not on any of the surveillance videos, and no one at the hotel recognized your picture or remembers seeing anyone in a wheelchair around the time of Mrs. Tremaine's death. But you and I both know you haven't been honest with me. The woman at the desk will return your personal items. Oh, and you've got a friend who's offered to give you a ride home."

Mendoza talked on his cell phone while I signed for my

things. When I was done, he rode with me in the elevator up to the ground floor.

"Keep out of trouble, Brandon," he said.

I rolled myself past uniformed officers to the reception desk, wondering who knew I was at the police station. I was about to ask the receptionist when I felt a hand on my shoulder. I glanced up.

It was Arthur. He looked worn out; his pleated wool suit was wrinkled enough for me to guess he'd slept in it. He pressed his right index finger to his lips and inclined his head toward the exit, indicating that I should follow him. My heart sank as I looked at the wall clock. It was a quarter past midnight.

The limo sat waiting in the parking structure, in the handicapped section. Arthur helped me into the backseat, then folded my chair and placed it in the trunk like a consummate professional. We drove out of the station onto San Vincente. Finally, Arthur broke the silence.

"I was concerned for your safety," he said, meeting my eyes in the rearview mirror. "Not to mention my own."

"Did the police question you, too?"

"I was interviewed at length."

"What did you tell them?"

"Things they would believe," he replied. "Because if I told them what actually transpired, I assumed I could be implicated in charges of kidnapping and extortion, or at the very least remanded for psychiatric counseling. Margaret would have wanted me to save myself from trouble. She was distressed after you left her office. She said she hoped things worked out for you. She would have wanted me to help you, which is why you're in this car."

I wasn't sure how he planned to help me, or how he could. I decided my best course of action was to say as little as possible.

"I'm very sorry for your loss, Arthur," I said. "I only met Mrs. Tremaine that once, but she seemed like a wonderful person."

"Thank you. That means a great deal to me. I've been with

Margaret ever since her affliction set in. She meant almost as much to me as my late wife."

We headed north on San Vincente and turned right onto Sunset, then drove without talking for a few blocks. When we passed La Cienega, Arthur pulled up in front of the Mondrian Hotel, just before the massive paneled wood doors that flanked the driveway sloping downward to the entrance. Brown, free-standing, immovable structures, they rose about four stories high, as overdone as the importance granted to the undistinguished white building nestled behind them, or the city in which it stood. I watched as "the beautiful people" entered and departed from the grand lobby on foot or in expensive cars, oblivious. One would never have guessed there had been a death that morning in this A-list-only hotel.

"I wanted to pay my respects," Arthur said, his eyes tearing.

"I understand," I said—although I didn't. Why pausing outside the hotel where his employer died was paying his respects was beyond me.

"They could never have charged you, you know," Arthur said, watching the entrance. "This hotel is under full video surveillance. Cameras at the entrance, the elevators, in every hallway. By the pool. On the roof."

"The detective who picked me up said as much. He knew I wasn't here last night."

"I'm surprised he was that forthcoming."

"I still don't know how she died."

Arthur turned to me.

"They didn't tell you? They initially believed she fell from the roof to the poolside, but weren't sure if she committed suicide or was murdered. She was murdered, all right, but she was never on the roof. She was never in the hotel, for that matter."

My heart began pounding in my chest.

"That's right, the surveillance cameras didn't reveal her entering the hotel either. Now I've seen the place near the pool where she landed. There's no possible way she got there from the roof. Surely the police reached the same conclusion. They say her bones were nearly pulverized. She had to have fallen from a much greater height. They're completely baffled."

"How do you explain it?"

"Clearly someone—or some *thing*—dropped her."

Suddenly I felt nauseous. I looked for the door release, in case I needed to throw up.

Arthur continued. "Before the start of Margaret's treatments she began having nightmares—terrible nightmares about Kyra and Desmond. She described them to me. They began as erotic but quickly turned disturbing, with both Kyra and Desmond being hunted by something that screeched like a bird and sailed through the air on great black wings. The dreams persisted after her vision was restored, even more violent and horrifying. Nothing seemed to help; not Valium, not Xanax, not Klonopin. Margaret asked me to sleep on the couch in her bedroom, for company. Each night her screaming woke me. Margaret was terrified that the demon was coming for them, that somehow it could see them through her eyes and she was leading it straight to Kyra and Desmond. He would tear them to pieces and it would be her fault."

My stomach heaved. I fumbled with the door handle. It wouldn't release until Arthur realized I was going to throw up. I swung the door wide and vomited onto the curb. He came around the side of the limo and handed me his handkerchief after I finished. I wiped my face, my vision swimming, my nasal passages on fire.

"You're having the same dreams," Arthur said. It was a statement.

Arthur closed my door and went back to the driver's seat.

"What happened last night?" I asked, dreading the answer.

"Yesterday morning, Margaret decided that she would not sleep last night. She made me promise to do all I could to help her stay awake. She hoped if she could break the cycle for even one night, the dreams might stop. It didn't make much sense to me. But we were both quite sleep-deprived, and there was nothing I wouldn't have done for her.

"We watched television downstairs until well past four, still dressed in our day clothes. Suddenly I noticed she was fitful, and realized she'd fallen asleep beside me. I woke her gently. She told me she needed something from her bathroom, and went upstairs alone. She promised she'd only be a minute. The next thing I knew, the sun was pouring in through the den window and I was alone. I ran upstairs. Margaret wasn't there. The window stood open. I called her name and got no response. I looked out the window, fearing she might have fallen and be lying below on the concrete. She wasn't there. I searched every inch of the house. Finally, I went back to her bedroom window. The lock had been bent upward, as if smashed with tremendous force. Leaning out, I discovered deep gouges in the wooden sill. I thought I was going mad.

"I calmed myself and called the police to report her missing, insisting that she must have been abducted. They told me they would send the next available car. When they got there, they informed me that the body of a woman matching Margaret's description had been found at the Mondrian Hotel. I took them upstairs to show them the damage to the window, and then they questioned me and I told them I couldn't explain it."

Arthur broke down, crying. If I had any lingering doubts about Kyra and Desmond, his words demolished them.

"Arthur, I am so sorry. You have to get me home. I need to warn them."

"No!" Arthur shouted. "You can't ever see them again. You'll lead that demon straight to them."

"Arthur, I know who the demon is. Kyra and Desmond told me everything. They need to know so they can defend themselves. And I'll never walk again if I don't see them. Tonight is my final treatment."

"That's the most selfish thing I've ever heard," he spat back.

"You'd risk their lives to walk again. I can see it in your eyes. I won't take you there, and I'll be damned if I'll let you go."

He hit the panel that locked all the doors, keyed the ignition, peeled away from the curb, and recklessly spun the giant car around into oncoming traffic, horn blazing, until we were headed west on Sunset, the opposite direction from where I needed to be.

Without thinking, I leaned forward from the backseat behind Arthur and caught my right arm in a sleeper hold around his neck, cinching my right fist with my left and squeezing hard against his throat, shouting, "Turn the car around or I'll break your neck!"

He fought me for a few moments, attempting to gouge my arms with his nails. I applied enough pressure to the chokehold to let him know I was deadly serious. He stopped fighting and pulled the limo to a screeching halt at the curb. I eased my hold.

"Let go of me," he growled.

"Not until you take me to the Villa Rosa."

"Then strangle me and have done with it, because I won't do it."

We'd reached an impasse, and time was quickly running out, if it wasn't already too late. I released Arthur.

"I'm sorry, Arthur," I said. "But I have to do this. Get me my wheelchair, and let me be on my way."

He did as I asked, glowering at me the whole time. But I couldn't be bothered with that. Once I was out of the car, he got back in, slammed the door shut, and sped off without another word.

The Villa Rosa was nine endless blocks away from where Arthur had stopped the limo. I took off rolling down Sunset without looking back, pumping my arms furiously against the wheels, harder than I'd ever done before. Sweat poured off my arms, dripped from my scalp into my eyes. I was in the bike lane; cars swerved to avoid me or I swerved to avoid them. Inattentive pedestrians and drunken partiers stepped out into the street without bothering to look around, assuming they had the right of way. I may have run over someone's foot but I couldn't stop to check. I passed King's Road and Sweetzer, passed Harper and the Body Shop, Crescent Heights and Laurel Canyon, the Griddle and the Rite Aid on the corner of Fairfax before I was forced to stop for a red light. The light took forever. When it finally changed, I forced my aching arms to take me across Fairfax, past Bristol Farms, to the Villa Rosa's front gate.

As I caught my breath, I looked up. Only a handful of apartment lights were on. One of them was Bethany's. Ray's apartment was dark. So was Kyra and Desmond's. Was I too late? Had they already left, believing I'd abandoned them? With a heavy heart, I reached up to the gate panel, punched the code, and buzzed myself in.

CHAPTER 13

I knocked on Kyra and Desmond's door and got no response. I knocked louder. More silence. Desperate, I tried the doorknob. It turned. I opened the door cautiously and peered into darkness.

"Kyra? Desmond? It's Brandon."

I listened a moment. I did not want to startle them if they were asleep. The only sound was the *whoosh* of traffic on Sunset, wafting in through the open French doors at the end of the hall. I reached inside to flip the light switch, then wheeled myself into the apartment.

The place was swept bare. Their keys lay abandoned on the kitchen counter. The Murphy bed was down, stripped of sheets and coverlets. A single broom I recognized from the storage cabinet downstairs rested upright on the wall near the empty closet. Tears flowed down my face as I sat in the barren apartment, and the ramifications of their absence hit me full force. The Fates had spoken. God had made His will perfectly clear. My only consolation was that Kyra and Desmond were safe from whatever was following them. I used that thought to get my emotions under control, and left the apartment.

I rolled out to the hall and discovered an envelope tucked in the jamb of my own apartment's door. A moment of hope that it was from Kyra and Desmond—before I recognized my mother's handwriting scrawled across the piece of mail which had been posted to me at my parents' address. The note read, "Thought you might want to read this. Love, Mom."

I rolled into my place and pulled the letter from the already unsealed envelope. At first, I had no idea who it was from. I had to read the vaguely familiar surname out loud several times before I finally got it. It was from the father of the frat boy from the accident. Just what I needed right then.

I headed for the bottle of Jäger and my glass on the counter, intending to drink every drop of alcohol I owned, and set myself up to read at the kitchen table, full glass in reach.

From beginning to end, I never touched a drop. This was not hate mail as I presumed. It was a farewell letter to a son he clearly loved. A father's desperate attempt to make sense of the inexplicable loss of his child. In it, he described his son's many achievements, including his aspiration to become a stage actor— he'd just been accepted to Yale Drama. He wanted me to know who his son was. What he could have been. And confessed that for some time he'd blamed me for his death. But now, to honor his son's spirit, it was time to forgive me my part in the accident, however great or small. His son had a big heart and would have wanted him to. He'd learned of my recent trials and prayed there might still be some chance for my full recovery.

Grateful as I felt, I knew it was exactly too late for his hopes or my own to come true.

Pummeled with emotion, I carefully folded the letter to place it back into the envelope, and that's when I noticed there was also a prayer card enclosed from his son's memorial. I read it with tears obscuring my vision. There was the haunting date of the accident again.

I turned the card over, not at all surprised to see the same familiar painting of that same haloed angel again: Head bowed, wings extended, hands steepled in prayer. Maybe that painting was one of those more commonly chosen? Or maybe it was all part of God's last big joke on me? Really, what were the chances?

I'm done, I thought. *I've just been absolved. I'll never be healed. What more on Earth is there for me to do?*

Just then my phone vibrated. It was a text from Bethany:

I HEAR YOU UP THERE. GET DOWN HERE RIGHT NOW!

I had nearly forgotten that Bethany had a stake in this, too. She'd loaned Kyra her passport and driver's license and been promised payment. I would have preferred to wait to speak to her, but now seemed as good a time as any to face the music. I picked up the Jäger bottle and headed downstairs. We might as well both get drunk, and decide what to do together.

"Where the fuck have you been? We've been waiting forever for you," Bethany scolded when she opened her door.

She was wearing a torn white T-shirt with red stains all over it, her hair pulled back in a bun. Before I could ask whom she meant by "we," Kyra popped her head out of the bathroom, her hair lathered and piled high.

"Hello, Brandon," she called, and popped back inside.

I heard water running, and realized she must be dyeing her hair to match Bethany's.

"Where's Desmond?" I asked Bethany, relieved.

"Long Beach," she said. "He went to take the last of their stuff."

Long Beach was the nearest shipping port, at least an hour's drive away. Bethany leaned close and whispered.

"They paid me. I've got two fucking hundred thousand dollars in a paper bag under my bed. I can't believe it."

My mind reeled.

"That's great, Bethany," I said, straining to keep my voice calm. "Listen. I need you to do something very important. Help Kyra get ready to come with me. Then pack a bag and check yourself into a hotel. Immediately. Please don't ask why. Just tell me you'll do it."

"If you say so," she replied, clearly a little surprised. "What then?"

"I'll text you tomorrow to get together, and explain everything when I see you. But hurry. There's not a minute to waste."

I watched Bethany help Kyra dry her now-red hair and help her decide on a cotton summer dress and sandals.

"How do I look?" she asked Bethany once she was dressed, as if she hadn't a care in the world.

Bethany looked her over and swept a few strands of hair from Kyra's face. I preferred her natural color, but the red dramatically brought out the gray and gold in her eyes.

"The red looks great on you," Bethany replied, turning Kyra toward her bedroom mirror to see. They looked similar now, except Kyra was about six inches taller than Bethany.

"You'll pass for me at a glance," Bethany offered. "The only problem is that my license and passport show me as five-five."

"We have a plan for that," Kyra said. "Thank you for everything that you have done."

"Come on," I said. "We gotta go."

"We need to take my bags," she said.

She indicated two black canvas duffel bags on the floor beside Bethany's closet.

"How long until you can be out of here?" I asked Bethany.

"Twenty minutes, at most," she said. "I just need to change. I have an overnight case already packed."

Of course she did.

"All right," I said. "Text me when you've checked in."

"See you tomorrow? Remember, you promised me an adventure."

I squeezed her tiny hand in mine, and ushered Kyra into the hall. I didn't know what tomorrow would bring. I needed to stay laser-focused on here and now.

"Tell me what has happened, Brandon," Kyra said as soon as we were in the elevator. "What has you so troubled?"

"Wait until we're in my place."

Kyra regarded me with her hawklike stare as I locked my apartment door behind us and set down the duffel bag I was carrying.

"Tell me," she demanded.

I considered how best to deliver the news in a manner that would upset her the least, fearing the last thing she'd wish to do after she heard it would be to finish my treatment. I began by telling her that Mrs. Tremaine was dead, then told her everything that had happened to me since we'd last seen each other. Kyra sat on the edge of my bed, displaying no reaction.

"Can I please use your telephone?" she asked when I finished. "I would like to call Desmond."

I handed her my phone. I could not believe how well she was taking it.

"It is happening, my love," she said when Desmond answered. "The name we do not say is close. Yes, Brandon is with me. Yes, I will tell him. I know. How far away are you? Please, drive safely. I fear he will come for you first. I know you do. I love you, too, with all my heart."

She handed back my phone. Desmond had already hung up.

"What did he tell you to do?"

"Anything and everything to stay alive. And to ask that you stay by my side."

"I will," I said. "How long did he say it would take him to get here? We need to go somewhere else. Someplace public would probably be safest."

"A public place will make no difference at all. Azareal is going to find us here. Before Desmond can return. Do you believe in predestination, Brandon?"

"How do you mean?" I asked, fear and adrenaline washing over me.

"I have visions, too," she said. "I knew from the moment we took this place that I would face Azareal again here. Just as I knew when I first met you, that you would be here to help me when I did. Desmond never wanted to believe that, but I had no doubt." I remembered the look that had crossed her face that day I'd paid for her groceries. I'd thought she was recalling my face from some commercial or supporting role she'd seen. That hadn't been it at all.

"If you knew the danger was coming, why didn't you leave sooner? Why bother with me? You could have run."

"That is not how it works. You cannot run from that which must happen. All you can do is face it, and surrender to the will of God. I knew when I first met Desmond in my mother's cabin that he would be my lover, and I loved him despite the visions I had then of what would come. I had no choice. Love cannot be denied. This confrontation was destined from the moment that Desmond and I joined. And we have been running so very long, my dear friend—longer than you could ever imagine."

I couldn't fathom what she was telling me. All I heard was that a demon was coming for us and there was nothing we could do to prevent it. Once again, she knew what I was thinking.

"You can choose to leave, Brandon. I will not force you to help me."

How could I live with myself if I abandoned her?

"Tell me what you want me to do," I said, surrendering all my petty thoughts and wishes to God. "I'll do it."

"You cannot help me in that wheelchair, Brandon. I need you whole," she replied. "And for that to be, I must make a difficult choice of my own."

"What choice?" I asked.

"The choice of how I will betray Desmond, the man who is my heart, my life, my soul. The man I would never willingly betray, unless it were to save his life. And that is why I will betray him. Because if I do not, he will certainly die."

"I don't ... what do you mean?"

"That is what Desmond would want, for me to give you the fig we have saved for him. But if I do what he wants, there will come a time, very soon, when the only way to save ourselves will be to use both figs. I have not seen exactly how, but the knowledge that it is so is deep and clear within me. If there is no fig for Desmond, he will die, for he will force me to take mine, no matter what it costs him. He knows this. It is why he did not want me to become too close to you. He thought he could prevent what must be. But the things I have seen are not so easily changed. I have explained to him that his death is unacceptable to me, but he does not care. He thinks that as long as I may have the fruit, and survive, it does not matter what becomes of him. He has made me promise that if the choice is between giving you the fig, or having you break my heart with joy so that I may heal you, I will use the fig."

I sat trembling as the implications sank in.

"You either betray him by using the fig and letting him die sometime in the future, or you betray him ... with me."

"Yes."

"You said this was your choice to make. What have you decided?"

"To save the fig."

There it was. She was asking if she could have sex with me at a time when she was convinced that Azareal was on his way to murder her. I desperately wanted to, had wanted to from my first sight of her, but how could I?

"You can try," I said. "But I can't—"

"Yes, you can," she said, cutting me off. "I promise."

She undid the straps of her dress and stood up, letting it fall to the floor. Quickly, she peeled away her undergarments and stood naked before me. Seeing her flawless, pale white skin, her supple hips I'd longed to grasp, those perfect breasts, was almost more than I could bear.

"Know that there must be love in what we do, but that the love I bear you is the love of friendship, the love of gratitude, not the love of the heart. That is Desmond's, and only Desmond's. Do you understand?"

"I understand."

"My poor friend," she said with a sad smile. "I know this

hurts you, but I also know that your heart will heal as well as your body."

I didn't trust myself to respond; instead I asked a practical question.

"Do you want me to stay in the chair or move to the bed?"

"There's no time to prepare the bed."

She reached forward to unclasp my belt and jeans, quickly tugging them away, then she lowered herself and straddled me, awkwardly placing her knees tightly around my dead legs, the confines of my cripple wagon forcing her to press her body down on mine. At first, I was loath to put my hands on her. Sensing my hesitation, she placed them on herself.

"Let go of your guilt," she ordered. "We do what we must. You have wanted me from the first, and now I offer you the love I am able to. Break my heart with love, my dear Brandon. Be healed, and help me save Desmond."

She tilted my chin up in both hands and kissed me deeply, sending lightning through my body. My manhood began to stir and slowly rise.

And so I let go of guilt, and lost myself in her; my greedy tongue devouring her mouth, my hands urgently exploring whatever part of her body they could reach. No, not exploring; I'd done that as Desmond in a dream. Now the dream was reality. I committed to memory all that I would never have again.

In moments, she had me inside her, and if I had not known that she was made for Desmond, I could have believed she'd been created for me. Everything was perfection—touch, taste, scent, sound, sight. She kept one leg on the floor and maneuvered the other beside me on the chair, gripping my shoulders with her hands and rocking her hips against me, taking me deeper and deeper. I wanted to go slow, draw out our pleasure, but that wasn't possible. Winged death was rapidly approaching, and I needed to bring on her tears. I would happily have died in her arms, reveling in the bliss of her embrace, but I could never condemn her to such a fate at Azareal's cruel hands. She had asked me to break her heart with love, and so I poured every bit of the love I felt for her into each touch, each kiss. I couldn't have done otherwise, anyway. My fingers moved between her thighs, stroking, caressing, teasing. Her breath grew labored. As her climax approached, mine built as well. I thought I might pass out from joy. She gyrated faster and faster, bucking and moaning and letting loose the sweetest birdsong. She shuddered with the force of her orgasm, every muscle constricting. And I came with her, shuddering against her.

I looked up. Tears were rolling down her cheeks. The tears burned as they touched my face.

Kyra slunk down from the wheelchair onto her knees, tugging me forward and turning me onto my stomach on the floor, forcing my shirt up, and laying her cool, damp cheek against the small of my back. Her tears touched me. My spine ignited with fire. The burning grew, scorching me.

"Stop," I cried. "It's going to kill me!"

She held me fast, ignoring my agonized screams. Finally, she pulled away and left me lying there. The pain faded; I heaved for air, then tugged up my pants and lay on the floor staring at her. She stared back, hawklike, her chest heaving, her legs drawn up close.

Suddenly, I was clinging to the roof of Desmond's Jeep as it careened northbound up the 405 freeway, glaring through hate-glazed eyes, flapping my wings wildly against the wind to shift the infernal machine off course, wanting to smash it against the stonework or flip it over, to tear the adulterer from its belly and rip out his heart with my bare hands. Then Kyra was holding my face, glaring into my eyes and shouting, "It is me you want, Azareal! Leave him alone. The choice to leave you was mine alone! Come take me back if you can!" I let loose a shriek of rage, loosened my grip on the hurtling machine, and soared up as fast as the wind would take me.

Kyra shook me awake.

"He is coming," she said, and sat back against the bed.

"I think you may have just saved Desmond's life," I said, quivering.

"Then whatever happens to me is worth it."

I saw she had gotten dressed, and asked, "How long was I asleep?"

"Only the briefest of moments."

Pain lived in my spine, so intense I could barely think straight. But I could feel my legs again, feel my knees and feet and toes, my pelvis.

"The pain will lessen soon," Kyra said, without my needing to ask. "And you shall walk. Let me help you back into your wheelchair."

With barely an effort, she lifted me into the seat.

"What do we do now?" I asked.

"We need weapons—guns, knives, clubs, spears. Whatever we can find. What do you have?"

"I've got some pretty sharp cooking knives in the pantry. There's a baseball bat in the closet. Is there anything different about you or Azareal that I should know? That we can use? What can hurt you?"

"My skin is many times tougher than yours. And he is many times stronger than I am, being from the first generation of Nepha. If you hit him, you must hit him many times harder. And if you stab him, you must stab him true. Other than our wings, these are the only differences that I know of. My mother always suspected that Azareal regularly ate the fruit of the Sacred Tree. If that is the case, he may be especially hard to kill. I wish now that Desmond had left me his gun."

"Guns sound like a good idea. Should we call the police?"

I had just been surrounded by cops and was disgusted by them. But right now I longed for their company.

"If they come, they will perish, and their blood will be on our hands. In the end it will be you and I alone. I have seen it. We can succeed, Brandon. I know it."

Kyra sounded confident, but I wasn't so sure. She unzipped Desmond's duffel bag and handed me a large, crude steel object.

"We also have this," she said. "Desmond calls it our alarm system."

At first, I couldn't recognize it. The object was extremely heavy, with big sharp teeth clamped tight to form a jagged, uneven seal, and a heavy, coiled spring inside. Then I realized it was a bear trap. It took both my hands and all my strength to pry open ever so carefully, to understand how the trigger mechanism functioned.

"Anything else?"

"Fire. My people use fire as punishment. It can harm us as it would harm you."

Maybe my liquor cabinet could be put to good use for a change. I went to my computer and typed in "How to construct a Molotov cocktail," and quickly had clear and easy directions. None of the booze I had was high enough in alcohol content. The bottles would work, but we needed gas and oil to make an effective incendiary mixture. The site listed the very best manner of wick.

"Do you happen to have any tampons, Kyra?"

"That is a need I have but once or twice per year."

I wheeled myself into the bathroom, hoping Felicia had left behind one or two in my medicine chest that I hadn't noticed. We were lucky; she'd left an entire box. I took them to the kitchen, collected several rubber bands, a BIC lighter, and, from under the sink, the plastic bucket the maid used for cleaning. Kyra helped me pour the liquor into the sink. We put the empty bottles and the kitchen knives into the bucket, along with the tampons and rubber bands, for Kyra to carry. I grabbed the bat from my closet and the bear trap from the bed, and rolled to the door.

"I've seen cans of gas and oil in the basement near the furnace," I said. "Let's hope they're still down there."

Suddenly, all of my apartment windows began to shake and rattle behind the drawn curtains. Barely four feet from where we were, we heard *thwump-thwump-thwump*—the sound of beating wings. We immediately turned off the lights. The maddening *thwump-thwump-thwump* continued. I wanted us to get as far away from the window as possible, yet we dared not move for fear we would be seen somehow, despite the curtains and the darkness. *Thwump-thwump-thwump.* I prayed Azareal would move on, presume we were on the run. But he remained outside, hovering. *Thwump-thwump-thwump.* The sound made my skin crawl. I gripped the bat, my heart pounding hard in my chest, prepared to swing should he somehow gain entry.

Without warning, the window shattered inward. Glass splinters rained to the floor. Two massive arms, fists bared, plunged through the curtains and tore them away, revealing Azareal, his black wings beating. Face raging, nude to the waist, his pale skin covered with raised ceremonial markings, dark hair straggling down to his chest, eyes dark as ink, his gaze locked on Kyra as he struggled desperately to get inside. But the heart-shaped cast-iron window grille blocked him.

He turned his gaze on me. We stared at each other—and at the same time I saw myself sitting frozen in my wheelchair beside Kyra through Azareal's deranged eyes. Only now I was awake, and completely disoriented.

Nothing will stop me from getting to her. She is mine.

I shook my head and was seeing Azareal through my own eyes again, watching him tear determinedly at the grille. It was starting to give way; plaster and brick chipped and crumbled as he yanked and wrenched with monstrous strength.

Kyra tugged my arm, breaking the spell.

"Let us go," she urged.

We dashed out of my apartment and rushed down the hall with our bucket of weapons, straight to the elevator. When the doors opened, we moved swiftly inside. I slammed the basement button.

"We must assume he will get inside soon," Kyra said. "We do not have much time. Are you sure it is worth that time to make these cocktails?"

"I don't think anything else we've got will slow him down at all."

The elevator door opened again, revealing the dank, smelly basement illuminated solely by dim safety lights. I flipped the EMERGENCY STOP switch, to keep it there. The only other way down was the stairwell. I steered through the ancient wooden door that led to it, pried open the bear trap with trembling hands, and set it on the ground beneath the bottom step, just in case Azareal came down that way before we went back up. I had Kyra unscrew the light in the stairwell. The trap became invisible in the dark. Wheeling myself back into the basement, I closed the wooden door and shot the bolt. I doubted it would hold for long—and prayed it wouldn't have to, that we'd be out of there quickly with what we needed.

The tubs of gas were full, along with several plastic bottles of oil, for which I will be eternally grateful to the Villa Rosa management. I poured two-thirds gasoline, one-third oil into each bottle exactly as the instructions indicated, leaving space for air, capping each bottle off and affixing an unwrapped, gas-soaked tampon with a rubber band to each bottleneck. There was enough gasoline to make six cocktails. I had just finished capping off the fifth when a sharp *clank* echoed beyond the closed door, followed by terrible shrieking.

Hideous pain flashed in my right leg above the ankle. I cried out, betraying our location.

"What's wrong?" Kyra said, looking worried.

"Pain in my leg. But it's not mine. It's his. It's gone now."

"I don't understand. How can his pain be yours?"

"If you don't know, I sure don't. It's really fucked up. But it's happening—and he's right outside that door!"

Azareal began smashing his weight against it. We grabbed our bucket of cocktails. The elevator doors closed as the basement door crashed down. I hit the fourth-floor button. Kyra squeezed my hand in hers.

She's mine, I thought. *She belongs to me.*

No, no, no, I told myself. *She's Desmond's!*

The thought enraged me. I shook my head desperately to clear Azareal from my mind.

"All right, here's the plan," I told Kyra as we ascended. "We're going to the roof. When Azareal comes, we smash him with these cocktails and hope he catches fire. If at any point we're lucky enough to get him down, we rush him. I'm going to slam him with this bat until I break every bone in his body. You stick knives in him as hard and fast and often as you can. Aim for vital spots—his heart, stomach, lungs, face, and neck. Slit his throat if you can. We don't stop until Azareal's dead. And then we do it some more, just to be sure."

I could barely believe I'd uttered those words, that it was me saying such terrible things. But I was determined to live, to protect Kyra or go down trying.

"Do you understand, Kyra?"

"I understand, Brandon."

I flipped the EMERGENCY STOP switch. We exited the elevator and proceeded to the stairs to the roof.

"Carry the bucket up first," I told Kyra. "Then come back for me."

Kyra sped to her task. I turned to face the stairs going down, ready for Azareal with the bat should he come up—that way or in through the French doors at the end of the hall. It occurred to me that I might have another weapon I hadn't considered. I closed my eyes and *willed my attention* away from myself to Azareal. For a moment I felt I was floating, formless ...

Then I was in the basement, struggling to remove the trap from a bloody leg. I remained as quiet as possible, and Azareal didn't seem to notice my presence in his pain-stricken mind—a vantage from which I could again see through his eyes. Getting a feel for the process in which he'd been seeing through mine. I shook off the vision as Kyra came down the stairs.

"He's still in the basement," I said. "Quick, carry me up."

"I do not think that you need me to, Brandon."

"What do you mean?" I said.

"Try to stand up. I believe that you can."

A thrill of hope pierced me.

"Really, Kyra?"

"I do. Try, Brandon."

Tentatively, I allowed my left leg to drop from the footrest. For the first time since the day of the car crash, I felt my shoe touch the carpeted floor. I dropped my right foot and raised my torso with my arms. Kyra smiled encouragement. I let go of the wheelchair. The forgotten muscles in my legs came to life; I was standing on my own power. My legs shook. Kyra put her arm around my shoulders while I steadied myself.

"Go up a few steps, Brandon. I'll stay beside you."

Together, we made our way upward, with me slowly raising my right leg, then my left, from one step to the next, leaning against the metal banister for support. At the top of the stairs, Kyra pushed open the door to the roof. The Los Angeles cityscape sprawled beyond us, more beautiful than I had ever seen it.

"I can't believe it. I'm walking, Kyra! I'm walking!" I cried with joy as we moved haltingly to the ledge, where I saw Kyra had placed the bucket with the bottles and knives.

"As I promised, Brandon," she responded. "But we must hurry."

I gently squeezed her hand in response and stopped her there by the ledge, overcome with emotion, then turned to face her. Our eyes met, and she offered no resistance as I slid my hands up along her arms to her bare shoulders and then *grasped my hands around her throat, enjoying the sudden terror in her eyes.*

I watched Kyra flail as Azareal choked her with my hands.

She scratched my face and dug her nails into my arms, her eyes wide, unable to understand why I was suddenly strangling her. My thoughts were still my own, but my body belonged to Azareal. I had to stop him before he killed Kyra. Distraught, I reached into Azareal's mind to see how he was controlling me.

Images of the Haven flashed in my head, of Nepha on their knees. Suddenly I understood that Azareal could possess others and bend them to his will. I knew this because he knew this. He had eaten the fruit of the Sacred Tree for so long that he'd developed the ability to see through the eyes of others and to control their physical bodies. Forbidden to interfere in the lives of men, he had used these abilities to control the Nepha, to cow all the males of the tribe and lie with the females. He had fathered so many of them, including the bride he was now strangling, who did not know she was his daughter. Kyra's mother had been manipulated by Azareal's malignant use of power, as so many of them had. None of the Nepha knew what the figs could do besides heal; they merely feared Azareal. But when Kyra ate the sacred fruit after Azareal lopped off her wings, it changed her, as it had changed Desmond when he'd consumed the fruit. Not only had the figs healed them, it sealed off their minds from Azareal.

For a time, this was all that was needed to hide the lovers from Azareal's hunt. But the burning spark of Kyra's healing tears was of the same essence as that in the fruit from the Sacred Tree, and connected Azareal to the people Kyra healed. That was the cause of the maddening nightmares. Some ceased having them when Kyra and Desmond moved on. Others Kyra helped were less fortunate. They went mad from the visions. Or were eventually tracked down and murdered by Azareal. The latest victim was Mrs. Tremaine. That's why they needed to keep moving, keep hiding.

Keep running. I will always find you. You are mine!

I watched, aghast, as Azareal tightened my grip on Kyra's throat until she lost consciousness. Finally, he released her and allowed her to fall from my hands. She lay crumpled on the ground at my feet. As quickly as I'd lost control of my body, it came rushing back. I sank shakily to my knees and felt Kyra's pulse. It was weak, but it was there.

Thwump-thwump-thwump.

I froze. That terrible sound. Looking up, I saw Azareal ascend over the far side of the building, wings fully extended, his face grim.

Thwump-thwump-thwump.

He landed hard atop the roof shingles, retracted his wings, and marched straight toward us, oblivious to the bloody bear trap wound in his leg. In a moment of clarity, I understood that he could not control both our bodies at the same time. He'd needed to release me to come and claim his prize. I was free to act.

I struggled to stand, my legs still weak from months of disuse, my ankles stiff, and limped over to the bucket. Grabbing the Jack Daniels bottle, I rummaged quickly for the lighter, glancing behind me to see Azareal sidestep an airshaft and tear off a satellite dish as he moved past it. Lighter in hand, I hurriedly lit the gasoline-soaked tampon, praying I'd made the things right. The tampon flared. I lobbed the bottle straight at Azareal, grateful for the strength in my arm. He stopped in his tracks. The bottle hit the roof and exploded at his feet, splattering flaming alcohol onto him.

It wasn't enough to stop him; he continued moving toward us. I brought out the bottle of Jamison, lit the fuse, flung it fast and hard. The lower tips of his wings caught fire. He flapped them, trying to extinguish the flames. They ignited further. He retracted his wings swiftly, folded them tightly, and reopened them. The flames had gone out. He began marching again. I grabbed the bottle of Jäger, lit it, and hurled it as fast as I could.

This time he was ready, having seen himself advancing through my eyes. A moment before the bottle hit he leapt airborne, then descended beyond the flames to land safely and storm forward.

I extracted the largest knife from the bucket, and stood as he came upon us and towered over me, glowering. He reached Kyra's unconscious body, raising his wings high and spreading his massive arms, each nearly as thick as my waist.

Attack me if you dare to, pathetic Son of Noah.

His thought echoed in my head. I forced him from my mind as best I could, and stabbed his bare chest with all the strength I could muster. The knife struck true, but Azareal's body was so strong, so inhumanly resilient, it deflected the blade, leaving merely a thin scratch of blood. I moved to strike again. He swatted me hard with his hand, smashing me backward over the ledge. I barely managed to hook my hands and hold on. My legs dangled in midair four stories above Sunset Boulevard. I told myself not to look down.

I struggled for a better hold on the stonework; the only thing saving me from slipping was the grip of my leather half gloves. A mere three feet away, the metal fire escape ladder from the fourth floor to the roof hugged the side of the building. It seemed like a mile. My fingers were going numb. I had to act now.

I swung my body by my hands back and forth like a pendulum, kicked out from the wall with my legs, twisted my hips, and hooked my right leg onto a rung of the ladder; had I missed it I would not have had a second chance. An instant later, I followed my leg with an instinctive release and grab of my right hand, painfully extending to snatch the rung, and swung from the ledge onto the ladder, hooking my left leg onto one of the lower rungs. I clung there for a moment thanking God, then scooted up the ladder.

Peering over the ledge, I saw Azareal reach down, scoop Kyra into his arms, and clutch her to his bare chest, mere yards away. She moaned, opened her eyes, looked up at him, and immediately began to struggle desperately. He squeezed her. She cried out. He opened his wings and ascended into the air. In that instant I knew he'd won. Kyra was doomed.

A shot rang out. Desmond had burst through the door and fired at Azareal. The bullet struck him in the back. Azareal contorted midair in pain as Desmond fired again, two shots into Azareal's back. Finally, he dropped Kyra. She landed hard on the roof. Desmond ran to her, firing his Colt once, twice, a third time. Azareal spluttered and landed on the opposite ledge, bleeding from multiple wounds, his eyes fixed on Desmond.

I had no idea what to do. Did Kyra survive the fall? Surely no human could have. Desmond quickly reloaded his Colt and took a position beside her. Azareal lunged up, flying at them in rage. Desmond fired again. Azareal reeled skyward and came down to perch atop the enclosure that led to the stairwell. With Kyra immobile, there was no other way off the roof for her and Desmond. How long could they hold on? How many bullets did Desmond have? Surely the gunfire would draw the police. Could they help us, despite Kyra's insistence to the contrary? I prayed she was wrong, but couldn't count on them arriving in time. I had to do something—*quickly*.

Then I remembered what was in my apartment.

I shimmied as fast as I could down the fire escape ladder to the fourth-floor fire escape, trusting my hands over my legs. Using the walls for support, I limped from the French doors to my apartment. I was momentarily disoriented as I stepped inside. Everything seemed a bit odd. I'd never been there standing up.

I moved to the duffel bags and unzipped Kyra's, revealing her severed wings. Repressing my revulsion, I peeled back the layers of plastic. I reached down past the feathers to something hard at the bottom of the bag, and lifted out a pointed bone shard about a foot long that looked like a stake. It must have become detached from the wings. This might penetrate hard Nepha skin, I thought, and slid the shard into the back pocket of my jeans.

I continued to search. A few moments later, I found a small

leather pouch about the size of my fist. I opened it expecting to find something dried out and prune-like. But the figs were fresh and ripe.

Yes, the fruit of the Sacred Tree, Azareal whispered venomously. *They are mine. You will bring them to me. Now!*

I struggled futilely as Azareal took control of me once more. He needed the fruit to heal his wounds, and I had led him straight to it.

He made me stand up, forced me out of my apartment. I stumbled down the hall fighting for control of my body, clutching the figs in my palm. I gripped the metal banister with my free hand, trying to stop myself. He made me pull myself forward up the stairs. Each step was a labored hell. He lifted my hand to the fire door, made me wrench it open. Filled with Azareal's blinding hatred for Kyra and Desmond, I stepped onto the roof.

Desmond was kneeling beside her, his Colt aimed at Azareal —who was perched on a nearby airshaft, positioned defensively behind a chimney stack. Desmond was clearly frustrated, trying unsuccessfully to get a bead on him, unwilling to leave Kyra's side even momentarily for a clear shot. I could feel the bullet wounds sapping Azareal's strength. He smiled demonically as I emerged from the shadows into the moonlight. Desmond looked to me.

"Where the hell have you been?" he shouted.

I wanted to warn him that I was a threat, but my voice wasn't under my control. Instead, I limped past him and Kyra, heading for Azareal to hand over the figs. It had been a long time since he'd eaten one, longer than even he had realized—before he left the Haven to pursue his prey. The fruit would heal his wounds. Heighten his strength. Make him nearly invulnerable.

"What the hell are you doing, Brandon?" Desmond called out over his shoulder, keeping one eye on Azareal.

Kyra had come to. She saw how I was moving, the empty look on my face. Her hand went to her throat and she cried out.

"Desmond! That is not Brandon!"

Desmond looked at Kyra, torn between gratitude that she was alive and confusion at what she'd said. I was also torn— between my own gratitude and Azareal's hatred. I was less than a yard from the glowering Nepha. He reached his hand out to me. I held forth the figs in my upraised palm.

"Stop him, Desmond!" Kyra urged. "Brandon is possessed. He tried to strangle me, before."

I heard the gun report, felt the bullet tear into my flesh; then a feeling of weightlessness as if I were floating, and the rush of warm air against my skin.

Thwump-thwump-thwump.

The sound was everywhere. I was back at my car crash on the 405, inside the crumpled steel, blinded by shards of glass. Unseen hands gripped me, pulled my body from the wreckage.

Thwump-thwump-thwump.

The helicopter propellers spun above me as it lifted off. Through a daze I heard the paramedic's voice. "Blood pressure is one-fifty over eighty; heart rate one-ten. Man, this kid reeks of alcohol." And in a flash I knew that what I'd feared was true: the accident was my fault.

Thwump-thwump-thwump.

My senses crashed back. I was under my own control, terrified to realize I was airborne, cradled in Azareal's arms. We were far above the roof. Instinctively I gripped his shoulder tight, to keep from slipping.

Gunshots rang out. Suddenly we were falling. Azareal opened his arms; gravity loosened my grip.

The roof rushed up to meet me. I smashed into it headfirst.

CHAPTER 14

I was dying. I lay on my back on the roof of the Villa Rosa, legs twisted beneath me at an impossible angle. I wasn't afraid. I'd been part of an amazing adventure. My only regret: I would not see how it concluded. I prayed that Kyra and Desmond would somehow defeat or escape Azareal and survive. But something cold inside me warned that if I were not there to help, they were doomed; he to death, she to servitude at least, more likely a lifetime of torture and abuse.

I opened my eyes. The moon shone high above me, haloed by clouds. I felt euphoric. I accepted the fact that I was dying, but I wanted to live. My left hand squeezed reflexively. *I still had the figs!* All I had to do was eat one. I tried to lift my wrist. It was broken. I tried to work my fingers; only my thumb was responsive. My forearm ached as I cocked it back and forth and tried to maneuver my elbow. It, too, was useless. I used my thumb to walk my hand, pressing the nail and pad against the rooftop and dragging my hand one painful inch at a time toward my face. At last my hand was just beneath my head, out of view. I hooked my thumb into the cloth of my shirt to hold it in place.

Then came the hard part. I needed to somehow turn my head on a neck I couldn't move and drop my mouth to my hand.

The fig was only inches away. If I could force my right elbow down, shove that shoulder up just a tiny bit, I might be able to wrench myself left enough to reach it. *Where was my chorus of angels?* I took a deep breath, imagined the deed accomplished, and went for it. Incredibly my head turned and fell just enough toward my left hand that I could fasten my lips to one fig, suck the fruit into my mouth, and gnaw it weakly with my ruined jaw.

At first, it tasted like any other fig. Then my mouth burned; my throat muscles spasmed when I swallowed. Fire wormed its way from my windpipe into my stomach and through my intestines, radiating through my arms to my hands, my legs, my feet, into my face and eyes and every pore of my skin. I felt as if I were being burned alive from inside. Eventually, the fire subsided to a tolerable level. I opened my eyes and lay quiet, breathing deep and knowing I was all right. Another miracle had saved me.

I rolled on my side, brought myself up slowly on my hands and knees, and stood, the heat of the fig still coursing through my body. I no longer felt Azareal or could see through his eyes. I felt no trace of his presence within me.

I heard the loud report of a gunshot above me, and realized that I had fallen much farther than I'd assumed. I wasn't on the roof. I was standing by the fountain in the Villa Rosa courtyard, near the entrance to the lobby. And the battle wasn't over. Kyra and Desmond must still be fighting for their lives.

I heard sirens. I looked at the front gate, and saw two police cars, lights flashing, pull up to the curb. Should I warn them?

"DO NOT INTERFERE!"

Azareal's voice exploded in my head. To my astonishment, the police cars pulled away from the curb.

We were truly alone. Kyra was right. There would be no outside help.

Another gunshot rang out.

I needed to get to the roof to give Kyra the second fig. Somehow, it remained in my hand undamaged. Pushing my fears aside,

I pocketed the fig and felt around my jeans for the bone shard from Kyra's duffel bag—my only possible weapon. It wasn't there. I searched frantically in the moonlit courtyard. Finally, I found it hidden among the irises. I hobbled with it through the lobby to the elevator and pressed the call button.

No response. I recalled that I'd flipped the EMERGENCY STOP on the fourth floor. I went up the stairs with my hand on the banister to guide me. I'd never been on them before. My legs still burned. By the time I reached the first-floor landing, I needed to pause for breath. Desmond had described the pain he'd felt after eating the fig, but hearing about it and experiencing it were far different. On the second-floor landing my stomach heaved; I fell to my knees and threw up. My eyes burned. My vision swam. As soon as I could collect myself, I wiped the vomit from my face with my sleeve and continued to the third-floor landing. By then, I could barely raise my legs. By the time I reached the fourth floor, my skin was drenched in perspiration and my muscles were in revolt, sending spasms from my toes to my upper thighs. I cleared the landing and was startled half to death by Ray, my inquisitive next-door neighbor, dressed in a garish satin bathrobe, clutching a flashlight and shining it straight in my face. The glare stung my eyes.

"Is that you, Ironside?" he whispered. He shone the light up and down my bent yet upright form, then back the way I had obviously come. I could sense his thoughts racing. "My God, did you just walk yourself up those stairs?"

"No," I replied, fearing for his safety and trying to sound authoritative. "You're having a drunken nightmare. Go back to your apartment, bolt the door, and don't come out until morning!"

Ray turned and ran back down the hallway with a look of blind obedience on his face. *Was he that scared or did I make him do that?* I wondered.

Gunshots rang out, startling me back to the task at hand. I had to get up there, fast.

Pushing through the pain, I hobbled to the last set of stairs leading to the roof, crawling up the final steps on my hands and knees.

As I was praying that I could summon the strength to stand and be of some use, I heard another gunshot just beyond the heavy fire door. Desmond screamed. I barreled through the door onto the roof. My eyes swiftly adjusted to the bright moonlight. Desmond and Azareal were nowhere in sight. Kyra was on the ground near where I stood. I went and knelt by her side. Her face was white; her skin cold as ice. I lay my hand against her chest; her heart was still beating. I fumbled in my pocket for the fig and pulled Kyra upright against my shoulder.

"You need to wake up," I whispered.

Her eyes fluttered open.

"Eat this," I said, holding the fig before her.

She stared blankly, giving no sign that she recognized me or the fruit or what I was asking her to do. I parted her lips and opened her mouth as one might a sick child's, and carefully fed her the fig. When she began to chew, I laid her gently down, got back on my feet, and went to search for Desmond.

I moved quietly across the roof, shard in hand, peering with trepidation into each airshaft, fearing that I was already too late. Should I have stayed at Kyra's side to protect her if Azareal returned? I searched the sky and saw no movement. Then I heard Desmond cry in pain at the far end of the roof. I rushed forward, clearing one final airshaft, and found them.

Azareal had Desmond pinned to the ground between his legs and was pummeling Desmond's bloody face relentlessly with his great fists. I lunged at Azareal, plunging the bone shard hard and fast beneath his wings, into his back.

The shard struck bone. Azareal flicked his wings, sending me sprawling backward; the shard flew from my hand and clattered away. I collapsed winded to the ground.

Azareal turned his head to regard me, his face contorted with rage—rage I, too, felt. I realized that I could still see through him, but his burning eyes could no longer see through mine. He turned back and closed his pale hands around Desmond's throat, to finish him.

Suddenly, I knew what I must do to stop him. I needed to possess Azareal as he had possessed me—and the fruit of the Sacred Tree had given me the will and the means to do it. In a way, Azareal had been training me all along. I'd seen through his eyes in the past. Now, I reached into his mind and, with barely an effort, took hold of his body. His hands on Desmond's throat were now my hands. I released their hold.

Realizing what I had done, Azareal looked at me, his teeth bared like a ferocious animal. Waves of hatred shot through my brain. For a moment I lost control. Azareal abandoned Desmond and rushed at me. I barely managed to regain my focus before he could reach me. I grabbed at his mind again, freezing him in his tracks and forcing him down on one knee.

Azareal fought me for control, lacerating me with murderous thoughts. I struggled to hold him. But now that I had him, I had no idea what to do with him—and he knew this. He smiled triumphantly as my confidence waned. I knew I only had moments before he used my indecision to break my hold; then he would tear me to pieces.

He reached into my mind and conjured images of my parents asleep in their bed, and of Bethany alone in some hotel room.

After I break you, I will kill them all. And Desmond. And take my Kyra back.

The intensity of his hatred shook me to my core. I lost control.

Azareal rose from his knees and towered above me, then reached down, grasped me by the throat, and lifted me in the air with one hand. I couldn't breathe. I struggled in his grip, beating his arm with my fists, kicking him with my legs. My vision blurred. As the final breath went out of me, I calmed and let go. Life began to drain from my slack body.

Beautiful voices sang in my head. I saw the Nepha through Azareal's eyes, assembled in the village square, led by Ruhamah, gazing at me.

And I saw Kyra rush headlong at Azareal and plunge the bone shard deep into his bare chest.

The shard struck true. I felt Azareal's pain and confusion as he realized what she'd done. All of the Nepha stood aghast as Azareal let loose a howl of agony and defeat. He dropped me to the ground; I lay gasping for air, sucking life back in.

Azareal fell to his knees before Kyra. She kicked him, hard. He fell backward, landing on the ground beside me, his wings spread wide beneath him as he clutched desperately at the shard, trying to pull it out and save himself. I watched Kyra step over him and smash her foot down on the shard, driving it deeper.

Azareal looked to me, his eyes pleading for me to save him, as if I might actually stop her. But he could no longer control me, and I wasn't about to show him mercy. He knew it was a piece of Kyra's wing that was killing him, a piece of her body he'd viciously severed—because I knew it, and I made damn sure he did.

Heaving for air, I crawled to the edge of the roof where the bucket lay overturned, drew out the final two bottles, and snatched up the lighter. I wanted to watch Azareal writhe as those infernal wings went up in flames. There was terror in his eyes when he saw what I planned to do. I liked that. I lit the fuses and got to my feet, my hands trembling as I gripped the necks of the bottles.

"No," Kyra shouted. "I forbid it."

Her hawklike eyes bore deep into mine.

Suddenly I was overcome with shame. Before I could respond, Kyra raised her foot and brought it down a final time against the shard. I felt Azareal die in my mind. Our connection was finally broken, and with it my vision of the Nepha.

Kyra rushed over to kneel at Desmond's side. Just as surely as my own, I felt her relief that he was still alive, felt her love flow out to Desmond, so deep it nearly broke my heart.

CHAPTER 15

*H*aving eaten the fruit once before, Kyra did not exhibit the same extreme aftereffects as the first time she was healed. Desmond's body was also resilient. His face was badly bruised, both lips were split, and one of his front teeth had been knocked out, but otherwise he seemed reasonably whole. Whatever damage lingered would be healed as soon as he and Kyra had the time and privacy to take care of the matter. Which wasn't now. The three of us worked tirelessly through the night, disposing of Azareal's body without remorse. This required a saw that we found in the basement, some gas from the tubs, and the furnace. When we were done, we placed the bones in several doubled-up garbage bags that Desmond took with him, along with their duffel bags, to his Jeep.

Come sunrise, the three of us said our goodbyes in the Villa Rosa courtyard. Desmond had given me my money, a large brown paper bag from Bristol Farms filled with crumpled cash. And I was back in my wheelchair, but this time by choice and not because I needed it.

"Why are you still leaving?" I asked. "Azareal is dead."

"The Nepha bore witness to my murder of Azareal," Kyra

responded. "I have broken the Sixth Commandment. Some of them will come to punish me."

"I doubt that, Kyra," I said. "I could feel what they were experiencing through Azareal. They realize now that he was controlling them against their will for a long time. They know that Azareal broke the Sixth Commandment many times himself. That he was trying to kill Desmond and had already killed Margaret Tremaine and others. That he would have killed you. I don't believe they will leave the Haven where they are safe, and expose themselves to the world. What they've seen of it must terrify them."

"I hope you're right, Brandon," Desmond said. "But we've been on the run a very long time, and made other enemies along the way."

Almost reflexively, I skimmed his mind to glimpse those enemies, and immediately wished I had not. Some of them were well-known men of power and celebrity, their bright, angelic faces masking savage predilections. Others seemed inhuman, no manner of men at all, capable of unleashing demonic designs on Mankind.

"So Kyra and I will stay on the move until we're sure we don't have to anymore," Desmond added, correctly interpreting the expression of horror on my face.

"I understand," I said. "Why by ship?"

"The distance from land makes attack much less likely," he explained. "We won't come ashore anytime soon, and never for any significant length of time. We'll be in touch when you can resume your normal life and let people know you can walk. I've gotten a wheelchair for us, to cement the use of your identity for a few months. And Kyra will use it when she needs to, in case the height difference between her and Bethany is called into question."

"Speaking of Bethany," I said. "She texted me while we were otherwise disposed. I have to get back to her. And at some point

I'll have to tell her I can walk. Do you have any suggestions for a reason I can give her?"

"I've been thinking about that," Desmond said. "Didn't you tell us your doctors weren't entirely without hope for your recovery?"

"Not entirely, but damned near it, and what little hope they did have kept shrinking as time went on."

"We can work with that. You'll have to remain in your wheelchair until you have your identities back. Once you do, why don't you and Bethany take a trip to the south of France. Little market town you may have heard about in the foothills of the Pyrenees, called Lourdes. Known for its miraculous healings. I'm sure you can make a convincing show of it there."

"That sounds like a good plan," I replied. "We talked about going somewhere."

"I think Bethany will love you, if you will love her," Kyra chimed in.

"I don't know about that, but we'll probably give it a try."

"I hope that you will," Kyra said. "And that you two will make many babies together."

"She can't make babies," I said.

"Yes, she can," Kyra shot back with that smile.

I knew better than to question her. If she said it was so, then it must be.

"We need to get moving, Brandon," Desmond said.

I wished they didn't have to, but I knew I couldn't convince them to stay.

"Thank you for saving my life," I told Kyra. "Literally and figuratively."

"Thank you for saving mine," she replied. "And for saving Desmond. We could not have stopped Azareal without you."

"Yes, thank you, Brandon," Desmond said. He hesitated, then went on. "I knew what Kyra said had to happen, and I tried to pretend there was a choice. It made me angry to think about it, and I was harsh with you when none of this was your fault.

For that, I'm sorry. If we'd done things my way, and Kyra had given you the fig to heal your legs, we'd all certainly be dead."

Desmond shuddered. Kyra reached out a comforting hand, giving his arm a gentle squeeze.

"Anyway," he continued, "if it had to happen, at least it was with a decent guy like you."

He hugged me close, then pulled back, involuntarily wincing from his as yet unhealed wounds. I followed them out to the Jeep where it stood at the curb. Desmond and I shook hands.

"Take care, Brandon," he said. "Don't spend all that money in one place."

I turned to Kyra.

"How long will I know what everyone around me is thinking?"

"The effects of the fruit will stay with you for quite some time," Kyra said. "Try to keep them as long as you can. Eat more figs. They remember the Sacred Tree." She kissed me on both cheeks. "Go and live a long, happy life."

It sounded like what it was; a final farewell from someone who expected never to see me again in this life. A few days ago, that thought would have given me devastating pain. Now, it merely brought a bittersweet ache. I had broken her heart with love, and in return she had healed mine.

"You, too," I said. "Take care of each other."

"We will," she said, and climbed in the Jeep on the passenger side as Desmond keyed the ignition.

Kyra waved as they pulled away. I watched them drive west down Sunset into the heavy morning traffic until other cars obscured them from view.

ABOUT THE AUTHOR

Steven-Elliot Altman is a bestselling author, graphic novelist, ADDY Award-Winning advertising executive, television writer-producer, and most recently a successful videogame developer, having served as the Games Director at Acclaim Games, and having won multiple awards for the games he has penned which include such titles as: *9Dragons*, which boasts 15 million players; *Pearl's Peril*, which boasts 90 million players; *Ancient Aliens: The Game* and *Project Blue Book: Hidden Mysteries* which Steve wrote, produced, and narrative designed for The History Channel, based on two of their hit television series. His latest game is *Terminator: Dark Fate,* based on the feature film.

Steve's novels include *Captain America Is Dead, Zen in the Art of Slaying Vampires, Batman: Fear Itself, The Killswitch Review, The Irregulars*, and *Deprivers*. He's also the editor of the critically acclaimed anthology *The Touch*, and a contributor to *Shadows Over Baker Street*, a Hugo Award-Winning anthology of Sherlock Holmes stories. Steve's also a proud member of the Science Fiction & Fantasy Writers of America, the Horror Writers Association and is the current Vice-Chairman of the steering committee of the Writers Guild of America's Videogame Division.

When Steve's not writing he is often playing social games with strange and wondrous people on and off of airplanes between Los Angeles, New York, and Berlin.

IF YOU LIKED ...

SEVERED WINGS, YOU MIGHT ALSO
ENJOY:

The Demon in Business Class
by Anthony Dobranski

Prospero Lost
by L. Jagi Lamplighter

Selected Stories: Horror and Dark Fantasy
by Kevin J. Anderson

OTHER WORDFIRE PRESS TITLES

Our list of other WordFire Press authors and titles is always growing. To find out more and to see our selection of titles, visit us at:
wordfirepress.com